CURTAIN CALL AT BROOKSEY'S PLAYHOUSE

A Lainey Maynard Mystery Series Book 3

LAURA HERN

Cover Design: Linda Boulanger

www.TellTaleBookCovers.weebly.com

ISBN: 978-1-61752-210-9

❀ Created with Vellum

PRAISE FOR THE LAINEY MAYNARD SERIES

"Just when I thought I had something figured out, there was a twist to make me rethink it. I lost a little sleep time over this one! Thanks for a terrific book! I am looking forward to many more from you."

— DONNA

"This book adds a delightful level of quirkiness with the murder mystery being solved. Lainey is a clever and hardworking detective, ready to tackle an unusual mystery involving DNA testing. The twists within the mystery are perfect."

— JIMMY B

"All the characters have spunk, especially the main character."

— FRANCIS P

WANT INSIDER INFORMATION?

JOIN HER NEWSLETTER!

Sign up for the latest news on previews, special offers, preorder information for the Lainey Maynard Mystery Series on her website:

www.laurahern.com

CONTENTS

INTRODUCTION

Present Day

Lainey plopped down in her favorite recliner and flipped on the TV. Her cat, Powie, jumped onto her lap as the first strains of The Late Show with Stephen Colbert began. It had been a long, exhausting day and she was more than ready to unwind.

"I made a lot of headway in the investigation today. Wish my Keurig wasn't on the fritz. I could use a mocha frappe," she said as she stroked the cat's back. Powie purred, squirmed a bit to get comfortable, and immediately began snoring.

"So much for listening to how my day went," she said quietly, looking down at the spoiled cat.

Lainey had been a fraud investigator for years and ten years ago, when her company relocated her from Houston, Texas to the tiny town of Mirror Falls, Minnesota, she wondered how many cases she would actually be given. To her amazement, her workload had become larger, not smaller.

She tried to listen to the monologue from the television program, but her thoughts kept re-visiting her first cases in Mirror Falls. Memories of meeting the Whoopee group and the Sullivans, the Governor's Fishing Openers, and, of course, Sarge, brought smiles and shivers at the same time. She paused for a moment before picking up her cell phone. "Call Francy," she said.

"Girl, what on earth are you doing calling me during the Late Show?" Francy demanded with a chuckle. "Is everything okay?"

"Has it really been ten years since I moved here?" Lainey said softly. A shudder ran down her spine as if someone had poured freezing water down the neck of her shirt.

"Come to think about it, I guess it has been. We've had a few adventures since then, haven't we?" Francy replied.

Lainey grinned. "Remember the Helvig case? That's when I first met you and joined the Whoopee group."

"I haven't thought about old Brooksey in a long time. Her murder rocked Mirror Falls, that's for sure."

"We didn't eat at the China Palace for months after that," Lainey chuckled. "Vera thought it was bad luck."

"I tried to tell her that the new owners had no connections to Ru Fong or Brooksey's Playhouse," Francy replied. "She didn't believe me until the McMurray's moved in next door to her."

"Do you remember when she took her famous coconut bars over to welcome them to the neighborhood? When they told her they were the new owners of the Palace, she got so flustered, she dropped the entire plate of bars!" Lainey's eyes were tearing up from laughing so hard.

"That was too funny!" Francy said. It took them both a minute to compose themselves.

"I was working when the call came in about the explosion. I think every officer on the force was there," Francy sighed. There was a seriousness in her voice.

"Things changed in Mirror Falls after that," Lainey said. "Was it worth the cost?"

CHAPTER 1
TEN YEARS EARLIER

The rain that had welcomed Lainey Maynard to Mirror Falls on Friday had continued all weekend. It was early Sunday morning when a sudden flash of lightning followed by a loud crackle of thunder jolted her awake. She jumped up from the recliner where she'd been sleeping.

"Jeepers," she said aloud, rubbing her eyes. "No one told me it rained so much in Minnesota." She stood up, stretched, and looked around at the stacks of boxes left to unpack.

Lainey had decided to make the move from Houston to Minnesota a few years after her husband passed away. Whether it was to try and hide from the many memories they had made during the eight years they'd lived in the Woodlands or if she was ready for a new adventure alone, she hadn't decided. Her boss said they needed an agent in the Twin Cities area, and she accepted.

She had done her research about the area and figured that while it was smaller than Houston and had less traffic, and she'd still have access to the theaters, sports events, arts festivals, and activities that she enjoyed. It wasn't until she had agreed to move and started looking for apartments online that her boss broke the news to her.

"Looking for an apartment, Lainey?" Her boss had inquired.

"I'm trying to see whether Minneapolis or St. Paul will be a better fit for me."

She could still see his face as he paused, then answered. "Oh, actually we're moving you a little bit west of the Twin Cities area. Mirror Falls to be exact."

"Mirror Falls?"

Lainey quickly typed the city into her Google search box. "Uhm, Mirror Falls is more than two hours west and north of Minneapolis."

"Business is brisk in that area and we need our best agent to handle it all."

Lainey grimaced. "I've known you for years, sir." She shook her finger at him. "Don't give me that spiel. What's the real scoop and why didn't you tell me sooner?"

Her boss shrugged his shoulders, chuckling a bit.

"You're right. It's much smaller than the Twin Cities. We have several key clients in the rural areas of Minnesota, and we feel that Mirror Falls is the best central location for you."

And that was that.

One of the first tasks Lainey completed once she arrived in Mirror Falls was finding a church to attend. She had decided to visit a Lutheran church located a few miles from her apartment. She showered, dressed, and looked up the website for the service time. She thought if it started at 8:15 a.m., she should leave earlier to beat the traffic and get a good parking spot.

She left her apartment at 7:20 a.m. and arrived in the church's parking lot at precisely 7:22 a.m.

"Guess it's going to take me a little while to adjust to

small town traffic," she said to herself, noticing that the Pastor, who was getting out of his car, waved at her. She got out of her car and walked over to meet him.

"I see you are eager to get to church today," he said, putting his hand out to introduce himself. "I'm Pastor Klein. Most people call me Pastor Pete. Welcome to our little church."

Lainey shook his hand.

"Thank you Pastor Pete. I'm Lainey Maynard. I guess I am a bit early."

"It's never too early to come to church." He put his hand to the side of his mouth to whisper, "Be careful not to make it a habit or Vera, our welcoming committee chairperson, will recruit you for something." He smiled and laughed.

Lainey grinned. "I'll be sure to watch for her."

As they walked inside, Lainey told him briefly about her move to Mirror Falls and that she was looking forward to getting to know the community.

"We'll do our best to help you get acquainted," he said, waving to someone coming down the hallway.

"Morning, Pastor Pete," the older lady said loudly as she hurriedly walked toward Lainey. "I see we have a guest this morning." She was still several feet away from Lainey when she put out her hand, dropping the grocery bag she was carrying. The bag hit the tile floor making a clanking sound that echoed in the empty hallway.

"Oh, shoot!" The lady exclaimed. "I hope the bag of coffee didn't spill out."

Lainey hurried over to help her, picking up a five pound coffee tin and the plastic bag.

"I don't think it spilled out. I'm Lainey Maynard. It's nice to meet you."

"I'm Vera Abernathy, the clumsy parishioner," she said with a big smile as she took the bag from Lainey. "I'm the

Welcoming Committee Chairperson. Thank you for picking up my can." She paused a bit awkwardly, then chuckled, "I meant my coffee can, you know!"

"You're most welcome," Lainey grinned. "I love coffee and am very glad we aren't picking up coffee grounds from the tile floor this morning."

Vera laughed. "It's for the coffee hour after church. The committee members take turns making the coffee and bringing bars or treats for everyone." She looked at Pastor Pete, stood closer to Lainey, then said, "Don't tell Pastor, but visiting at coffee hour is the highlight of our Sunday morning!"

"Now, Vera, I'm sure you meant that after my *sermon*, visiting is the highlight, correct?"

They all laughed.

"Would you please help me get the coffee pots brewing?" Vera asked.

"I'd love to," Lainey replied not wanting to hurt her feelings. She glanced at Pastor Pete who was grinning.

"I told you Vera would put you to work," he said almost gloating.

Lainey nodded, smiled, and followed Vera to the kitchen.

"Now, tell me all about you, your husband and family," Vera said as she began taking large coffee pots from the cabinets and placing them on a counter.

"I'm an insurance investigator and moved just a few days ago from Houston. I'm a widow and have no children, so there isn't much to tell."

Vera stopped moving coffee pots and instantly had tears in her eyes as she turned to face Lainey.

"I'm so sorry you're alone! I lost my dear husband, too." Her voice broke for a second, then she wiped a tear that had rolled down her cheek.

She gave Lainey a big hug and said, "You have to meet my daughter and Della."

"I'm sorry if talking about my late husband upset you or brought back sad memories. I would be happy to meet with your daughter and what was the other person's name?"

"My daughter is Francy and Della is the other person in our little group. You're going to fit right in!"

Vera was finishing the coffee pots and Lainey was cutting the bars and arranging them on trays when another loud voice sounded. Lainey looked up to see someone running toward them, carrying many bags and a desk fan.

"Mom, I told you to wait for me to help you with those heavy pots," the lady almost shouted.

"I've got Lainey to help me. She's new and is going to join our group." Vera answered, putting her hands on her hips.

This must be Vera's daughter? What was her name again? Fran?

Lainey walked forward to offer to help her carry something.

"Thanks, but I've got it," the woman said.

She put the desk fan and the bags on the counter, then straightened her blouse and raked her fingers through her hair.

"You know your back is going to hurt if you've been lifting those pots again," she cautioned. Then she focused her gaze on Lainey and put out her hand.

"I'm Francine, Vera's daughter. Please, call me Francy."

Lainey nodded and shook her hand.

"It's nice to meet you. I've only met Vera this morning. She's a great Welcoming Committee Chair." She winked at Francy.

"Oh, I know it. There isn't one visitor in the last seventeen years that my mom didn't welcome."

Vera smiled wide. "It's my gift and I take it very seriously!"

Lainey looked at Francy and grinned.

"Francy, I told Lainey that she needs to join our group and meet Della right away. When is our next dinner date?"

Francy saw the curious look on Lainey's face and quickly added, "Mom, did you happen to ask her if she *wanted* to meet with us?"

Vera waved her hand at Francy as if she were batting a fly in front of her face. "Of course, she does. You like to play cards, don't you?"

"Well, yes I do," Lainey answered, looking from Vera to Francy. "But if you need to ask Della, I completely understand."

"Piddle!" Vera exclaimed as she dismissed that thought. "Francy and I like you. Della will, too."

"It's useless to argue with my mom. If she says you're perfect for our group, then welcome to the Whoopee group!" Francy said smiling.

"What did you call your group?" Lainey said as she tried not to giggle out loud.

"You'll soon see," Vera said. "Francy, where are we meeting next week?"

"We're going to grab a bite to eat at Babe's at 5:15 on Tuesday, then go to Brooksey's Playhouse. It's the last day to see Harold's Fantastic Cow," Francy answered. "I'm sure we can get another ticket."

"What is *Babe's*? Is it in Mirror Falls? Is there a dress code?" Lainey asked.

"Heavens no! If they don't like the way I dress, then I'm happy not to support their restaurant!" Vera said somewhat indignantly.

"Yes, both places are in town. Babe's House of Caffeine is our local favorite and only place to get specialty coffee--like my favorite, caramel macchiato. Brooksey's Playhouse is our local theater group. Both are downtown about a block or so from each other." Francy said.

"My downfall is a skinny mocha frappe with no whipped cream," Lainey answered, smiling and licking her lips.

"See, I told you she'd fit right in." Vera smiled.

CHAPTER 2

It was still raining Monday morning. Lainey had been up early, making sure her computer network, modem, router, printer, and laptop were working properly. Finally, convinced that all wires, lines, passwords, and codes were entered correctly, she tried to login to her work server.

Blazing across the screen were the now familiar words: **Updates loading... server not responding. Contact administrator.**

She left a message on the Tech Hotline stating she needed urgent assistance. The time showed 3:52 a.m.

"I'm sure Tech Services will love being greeted Monday morning with my message!" Lainey mused, turning to her cat, Powie. "I need more coffee this morning. How about you?"

Lainey had always been a bit impatient and waiting for 8 a.m. to arrive in order to start the long, often drawn out process of getting all her programs up and running was simply boring.

She turned on the local news to see that more rain was forecast, and she began surfing the channels. Finally, she found the PBS channel running an Agatha Christie favorite with Hercule Poirot.

"Coffee and Poirot! All is good in the world." She sat in the recliner and fell quickly asleep.

She awoke to her phone ringer playing *Under the Boardwalk*. It was tech support. Within a couple of hours, her computer was restored, and she was checking emails. She reread one that was flagged urgent and printed it. As requested in the email, she called her boss for more details.

"Good to hear your voice, Lainey!" He said. "I thought maybe you'd drowned or got lost while poking around Mirror Falls."

"Ha, ha. Very funny," Lainey was not amused. "I've been on the phone with the Tech Department trying to get my computer fired up."

"I see," he replied, sensing that she wasn't in the mood for jokes. "You're calling on the Herman Helvig assignment?"

"Yes, what's the problem?" Lainey had her pen and paper ready to jot down the details.

"Herman Helvig is the retired President of the Mirror Falls Bank and Trust. He still sits on the Board of Directors. He grew up in the area, is respected among the business community for his intuitive approach and the ability to turn a failing opportunity into a thriving and profitable one."

"Got it. He has business savvy and is well-known in the community," Lainey recited.

"Fifty-one years ago, he married Brooks Olsen, daughter of a local family of farmers. She was known around town as Brooksey, was a stay at home wife, had no children and over time became a beloved philanthropist in the area." He paused to let Lainey catch up on her notes.

"How does a possible murder fit into this?"

"Mrs. Helvig was found dead two weeks ago of an apparent heroin overdose."

There was silence on Lainey's end of the call.

"Lainey? Did we lose the phone connection?"

"No, sir, I wasn't expecting to hear about an overdose of anything," she replied.

"There was a key person life policy written on Brooks about a month ago."

"How much did Herman inherit?" Lainey asked.

"That's the root of his call to us. His wife was the sole owner of a small theater… let me get the name… Brooksey's Playhouse."

Lainey shivered. "Are you sure it's called *Brooksey's Playhouse?*"

"Yes, why?"

"I'll let you know after I do more research."

Her boss cleared his throat and continued. "The policy was written with someone other than Herman named as beneficiary. And it was for a million dollars."

Lainey paused in thought. "Who's the beneficiary?"

"Jillian Blumpkist, the manager of the Playhouse."

"The entire million goes to this Jillian? I can see why the husband is upset."

"Can you get in contact with Helvig this morning? It sounds to me like he feels his wife was a victim of foul play. And if it turns out to be true, the policy is void."

"I'll get right on it. Anything else I should know?"

"That's where you come in. Your job is to find out what else we need to know before paying this claim."

"Send me any and all information you have. I'll contact Helvig as soon as possible."

"Thanks, stay in touch. Let me know if you need anything," her boss said before hanging up.

Is it a coincidence that I'm going to Brooksey's Playhouse this week? Could Vera or her group be involved?

Lainey regrouped her notes and called Helvig. The

answering machine had a lady's voice and she wondered if it was Mrs. Helvig. As she was leaving a message with her company name and phone number, someone hurriedly picked up the phone.

"Hello? Hello? This is Herman Helvig."

"Hello, Mr. Helvig. My name is Lainey Maynard. You called my company to investigate the death of your wife. I am very sorry for your loss. Is this a bad time to be calling you?"

"Thank you. No, I want to speak with you in person. When can you come?"

Lainey paused to check her calendar. "Would later this afternoon or evening be convenient for you?"

"Come to Brooksey's after 8 p.m. The playhouse will be empty by that time."

"Yes, sir. I will be there. Here is my phone number in case something comes up and we need to reschedule."

"I have your number and I will not need to reschedule. It is urgent that I speak with you as soon as possible."

Lainey hung up, wondering why it was so important to Herman for the theater to be empty when they met. She plugged Brooksey's Playhouse address into her phone GPS. It was a ten-minute drive from her apartment. She decided to research the theater and freshen up before going to see Mr. Helvig.

The building had quite a checkered past. During the late '30s and '40s, the Midwest was a favorite hiding place for bootleggers, gangsters, and bank robbers. The small population, cold weather, and even corrupt law enforcement officials during those years made it easy for criminals to seek sanctuary and run their operations. These included John Dillinger, his girlfriend, and Al Capone. Even Bonnie and Clyde roamed the Midwest during their heyday.

Lainey sat back in her chair and rubbed her eyes. Her

iPad didn't have the best background light for reading. She blinked a few times and continued scouring the online articles. After scrolling through tons of newspaper archives, one post caught her eye.

"Two Capone gang members arrested at Mirror Falls brothel," she read aloud.

Mirror Falls had a brothel? What else is my new hometown known for?

The article stated that police had arrested two members of Capone's gang who were engaged in illegal activity with prostitutes at Miss A's Stallion Saloon. Lainey quickly opened another search window and typed the saloon name. Seems the saloon was the most popular place in town. Men were frequently seen coming and going at all hours of the day and night. She read on to find that Miss A's name was Ai Jiao Ju, which meant *lovable fine daisy flower* in Chinese.

There was a black and white picture of a brick, two story building with police officers and men in handcuffs walking toward what looked like an old paddy wagon. Lainey kept wondering how this was related to the Brooksey's Playhouse. Suddenly the newspaper words seemed to jump off the page into her lap. The saloon had been closed down shortly afterwards and the building had been turned into a theater by the city!

She looked at her watch and realized it was time to leave for her meeting. She turned off her iPad, got into her car and headed to the Playhouse. She had many questions to ask Helvig about his wife and many more about the theater. She arrived fifteen minutes early, walked inside, and was surprised by the regal appearance of the foyer.

The high ceilings were painted with exotic designs and ornately trimmed with gold leaf patterns that sparkled. There were two spiral staircases on either side of the foyer, and polished, hand-carved wooden pillars supported the grand structure. Red velvet draperies with gold tassels framed the tall windows to just above the floor. Playbill posters graced the space between them. There was a musty old smell that caused a tingle in Lainey's nose.

"You're an hour late!" A gruff male voice said loudly, startling Lainey back into reality. "Do you have the information?"

Lainey looked bewildered.

"I'm Lainey Maynard," she said as she put out her hand.

"Yes."

"I'm here to get information from you concerning your wife's death. What were you expecting me to give you?"

"Oh, nothing, nothing," he stammered as he turned his back to her. "Follow me. Let's talk in the back office."

He was an older man of medium height. His hair, while receding from his forehead, was meticulously styled, giving him a very classy look. He was wearing an Ascot Chang designer polo shirt, a sleek pair of casual dress slacks, and a pair of Ferragamo shoes.

He certainly knows designer fashion and wears it well.

He walked briskly, giving the impression he was in very good shape.

Helvig walked past the ticket booth and bar area, through the great doors leading into the main floor theater, and down the sloped middle aisle toward the orchestra pit. Lainey, hurrying to keep up, tripped on one of the many ripples in the faded red carpeting. Somehow she managed to keep her balance and noticed that Helvig never looked back to see if she was following.

He approached a black door to the left of the orchestra pit, reached into his pocket and pulled out a large set of keys.

"I bet it's difficult to see that door when the lights aren't on," Lainey said as she waited for him to find the correct key.

"That's the point," he grunted. "Only I have access to it. The door closes and locks automatically."

He opened the door, walked inside, and flipped on the light. They entered a short narrow hallway that led to a single door forty feet away. Helvig headed to the next door, fiddling with his keys once again. He abruptly turned to face Lainey just shy of the second door.

"What you see inside and what we discuss is strictly off the record," he stated bluntly. "Otherwise, you can leave now."

Lainey nodded, wondering what was behind the door that would cause him such concern.

He turned, opened the door, and this time motioned for her to enter first. She began walking down a tightly curved rock staircase.

This is like walking down the stairs of a lighthouse.

The walls looked as though they had been chiseled out of an iron ore mine. After what seemed hours, the stairs ended abruptly in front of a small iron door.

Once more, Helvig dug out his keys, pushed Lainey aside, and opened the heavy door. The extremely overpowering scent of incense or some pungent urine-type odor immediately irritated her nose and throat with a hot, burning sensation that caused her to start coughing and choking.

"What is that putrid smell?" She sputtered while choking.

Helvig, ignoring her question, flipped on a light switch, and closed the door.

"This room was built with little ventilation and it wasn't meant to be a place where people stayed for long periods of time," he said.

Once she stopped coughing and could look around, what she saw shocked her. The room resembled photos of old opium dens she had seen in history books. There were no windows or other doors. A single light bulb hung from a brown, cobweb-covered electric extension cord string strung across the ceiling. It cast a dim, scary glow to the room. The only furniture were two very old wooden chairs, several stained yellow straw or bamboo mats on the grimy cement floor, some grungy soiled pillows, a few hat-type hangers on the wall, and one old dresser with four drawers. Lainey gasped.

"This is an old drug den!" She exclaimed angrily at Helvig. "You brought me to a drug den? Open that door immediately. I want no part of this!" Her eyes flared and the glare she gave him could have melted steel.

"Relax, Ms. Maynard. I'm not a drug dealer and you're in no danger," he said, amused at her rage.

It dawned on her that while she was coughing and choking because of the stench held within the walls of this dingy little prison, Helvig never flinched, coughed, or choked.

"It seems you are immune to this room's unique odor," she said sarcastically. "Come here often do you?"

He flinched at the remark, then sat down.

"Sit down," he said calmly. "I won't keep you here long."

Lainey stood her ground. "I'm not sitting, lying, or touching anything. Talk fast. You have one minute before I call 911."

"I had to bring you here to see this firsthand," he began. "Otherwise, you wouldn't believe the story."

"You're out of time. I've seen it. We can talk upstairs. Now open the door!"

Lainey continued to glare at him.

Helvig paused briefly and looked intently at her as if trying to decide whether she was serious or not. He got up and walked over to the door. The decades-old hinges groaned with an eerie, dreadful screeching noise as if the room were crying or pleading for them to stay. Lainey didn't remember hearing any sound when it was first opened, and it made her skin crawl.

Helvig turned to face her.

"I'm warning you," he stated flatly. "Anything you see here is off the record." He turned to start up the stairs.

She glared at him and followed in silence.

When they were back in the theater, Lainey felt she needed to shower, change her clothes or something. That horrible smell lingered in her throat and nose. She doubted if she would ever forget it.

"Now, we can talk in the front office," Helvig said as he walked up the middle aisle. Lainey followed, feeling a bit queasy and mad at herself for that reaction.

Crap, Lainey, pull yourself together! You're tougher than this! It was just a smelly room for crying out loud.

The front office was behind the ticket window and Lainey was glad to be above ground sitting in a padded office chair. She was very cautious not to show Helvig how relieved she was.

He sat down behind a small Chinese-style black cherry desk. Still mad about the hideous room she had just seen, she stared at him with her arms crossed.

"I hope I didn't scare you too much," he said. "I know how fragile women can be." His demeaning tone only infuriated her. It was obvious how she felt was of no concern to him.

Fragile? He thinks I'm fragile? Buddy, you just barked up the wrong tree!

A lightning bolt of anger raced up her spine.

"Look, Mr. Helvig," she said with the scolding voice of a principal reprimanding a student for cheating on a test. She leaned forward putting her hands on the arms of the chair and stated boldly, "I'm not here to debate your chauvinistic view of women or crumble because of some stinky opium room you frequent. I'm here because you claimed your wife was murdered. Tell me your concerns or I'm leaving."

Helvig was obviously startled by her bluntness and without missing a beat, he said, "That room is part of the history of this building and plays a huge part in why I believe my wife was murdered."

Lainey sat back in the chair. Her eyes were still fixed on Helvig's face, waiting for him to continue.

His demeanor softened as he picked up a small green globe that was resting on a carved teakwood pedestal near the right corner of the desk. He admired the globe, turning it around in his hands, then he sighed and began speaking.

"This is jade. It's been called the *Stone of Heaven* and, in Chinese history, it symbolized nobility, virtue, honor, and wisdom," he said, carefully putting the globe back on top of its pedestal.

Where is he going with this?

"Jade is really two different gemstones, nephrite and jadeite. Both are so hard they can't be carved or cut. They must be worn away by abrasion with specially designed tools. To form jade into a shape is time-consuming and very labor-intensive. It requires extreme patience over a long period of time," he said as he looked at Lainey.

"I appreciate your knowledge, but why is this important?" She asked.

"Just like a piece of jade, this building has been worn away over its lifetime. This magnificent structure has its roots in Chinese history, drug smuggling, and human trafficking."

"I did a little research on this building and knew that it was a brothel at one time," Lainey replied, hoping to sound knowledgeable. "Miss A's Stallion Saloon, I believe."

"Yes, it was. It became a favorite of not only American gangsters, but a few Chinese organized crime bosses as well. It's been said that Miss A belonged to a high-powered mob family in China. That room you saw is the last remaining section of an underground tunnel that housed young Chinese girls who had been stolen from their families and brought by ship to America."

Lainey relaxed slightly as he talked. She was intrigued and somewhat disgusted by this news.

"Did the police know she was involved or arrest her?"

"Many of the police in those days were corrupt. The chief of police visited Miss A quite often. And, in return for her services, made sure law enforcement looked the other way."

Lainey nodded.

"After the saloon was shut down, the building sat vacant for decades. The days of Dillinger and Capone ended, the town was no longer gossiping about prostitutes, and the building slowly crumbled. The city's water department found the tunnel system while replacing the sewer lines in the '90s. It was decided to fill them in and forget they existed."

"Why was the room below left untouched?"

"It was built especially for Miss A. I discovered it when I bought the building for Brooksey."

Lainey was silent for a moment, trying to piece things together.

"How did you get a key?"

Helvig grinned wide and laughed. "When I purchased this building, I took ownership of everything connected to it. Seems Miss A had a long-forgotten safety deposit box. The key was inside."

Lainey stood up and paced around the office for a moment. Thoughts ran rampant through her mind.

Hidden rooms, human trafficking, drugs. Why is he telling me this? What's he hiding?

Suddenly she realized he had been watching her pace and she quickly sat back down.

"Why did you hire my company? Nothing you have told me ties into your wife's death or the key person life insurance policy you didn't inherit," she stated boldly. "It's time you level with me."

His smile disappeared and his mouth turned into a small, thin line. She could tell he wasn't used to her bluntness.

"I will not be talked to..." his voice trailed off before he could finish his sentence. She could see he was rethinking his words and he was straining to control his temper.

"My wife was a kind, gentle soul, and would help anyone who asked her. She championed the mission of bringing the arts to Mirror Falls and, to her credit, she accomplished that. But her naïveté was her downfall. And because of that, she was frequently taken advantage of. My position in the town allowed me to protect her many times."

"But not this time. Is that what you're saying?" Lainey asked, wishing she hadn't been so quick to blurt that out.

He paused and looked again at the jade globe. "Not this time."

There was a long silence between them. Neither one was wanting to speak first.

"This playhouse was Brooksey's pride and joy. When she first opened it, she would advertise for locals to audition and put on three or four community theater plays a year. Simple, fun, and she knew I would finance anything she needed," he stopped abruptly and once again his demeanor visibly changed.

"Out of the blue, Jillian Blumpkist appeared in our life. She called, she dropped by the playhouse, and sent notes of praise and gratitude to Brooksey. My gut said she wanted something, and I warned Brooksey about it. But she didn't believe me," he said sarcastically.

"Jillian is the manager of this place, isn't she? Why did you hire her?"

Helvig slammed his fist on the top of the desk.

"I didn't hire her! Brooksey thought she would be an excellent prodigy to continue the playhouse's mission after she retired. I found out when Brooksey asked me to write a payroll check to her." Sensing Lainey's alarm at his angry outburst, Helvig took a deep breath, sat back in his chair, glanced upward, then back at her before speaking.

"Please, excuse my harsh response. I'm still trying to cope with the death of my wife and my feelings are a bit on edge."

Lainey nodded. She had been silently studying the man's facial expressions and body language. He was right-handed. Her years of training had taught her that if you ask a right-handed person a question about an event or situation he is familiar with, he will look upward and to his left if he's truly accessing his memory. Helvig had looked upward and to his right, which meant he was accessing his imagination while trying to create a believable answer.

He's lying to me. But why?

"Your wife knew of your dislike for Jillian, yet she hired her anyway and made her the beneficiary of a large life insurance policy. Why would she do that?"

"Brooks had a tender heart and believed every sad story anyone told her." His eyes blinked rapidly several times as he spoke. "Jillian knew this and invented some sad story about her parents being drug dealers. She said they overdosed when she was a small girl and she spent years being moved from foster home to foster home. Brooks felt sorry for her and was trying to help her."

"Why didn't you believe Jillian's story?"

He pushed back his chair as if he were going to stand up. Instead, he opened a side desk drawer and pulled out a brown folder. He laid the folder on his desk and looked directly into Lainey's eyes.

"I'm a successful businessman and have a keen sense, an

intuition that has served me well over my long career. Frequently, people have tried to take advantage of Brooksey's generosity, and each time I had to intervene to protect her and our fortune." He paused and picked up the folder. "When I met Jillian, I immediately had an uneasy feeling. I retained a private investigator and asked him to get information on her." He leaned forward to hand her the folder.

"Inside you will see the results of his investigation and why I think she murdered my wife."

There was an awkward silence in the room as Lainey took the folder from him.

"This might take some time to go through and it's getting late," she said as she stood up. "I'll call you when I have more questions."

Helvig stood up and walked to the door.

"You have my phone number. I'll expect your call."

She walked through the grand foyer with Helvig following behind her. She abruptly turned to face him before going outside.

"Before I leave, I need to ask about the report that said your wife died from a heroin overdose. How long had she been using?"

Startled, he paused slightly before answering.

"Brooksey would never use drugs of her own free will."

Lainey stood still, trying to process that strange response.

Her own free will? Is this why he thinks murder?

"One more question. When I first arrived, you asked me about information I was to bring you. What were you expecting?"

"Information about the next touring group Brooksey had scheduled at the playhouse, that's all."

She could tell by the stony look on his face he wasn't going to tell her the truth. She stood for a moment longer, watching him.

"Thank you for calling our company. I'll be in touch with you soon," she said as she walked outside into the crisp night air.

You will definitely be hearing from me!

As she drove home, her mind kept replaying the scenes from the theater, the putrid odor of the hidden room, and the odd conversation with Helvig. She glanced down at the folder sitting on the seat next to her.

"It's going to be a late night," she said aloud.

CHAPTER 3

When Lainey got home, she fed the cat, changed into her favorite pj's, and sat down at her desk to look through the folder Helvig had given her. She found three sets of stapled papers with three pages each. Each set had lines that were blackened out by a marker, which made her even more curious and suspicious.

"Why would Helvig give me a detective's report to examine that had information redacted?" She said to Powie, who was lying in her lap, purring loudly. "Sounds fishy to me," she added.

The detective agency's information was blacked out as was the name of the private investigator and the date of the report. She began reading and writing notes for herself.

Jillian A. Blumpkist was born in 1979. She was found in a trailer home in southwestern Stearns County when she was less than a month old. The mother had overdosed on heroin and no birth records for her were found at area hospitals. CPS had taken custody until she was adopted by Joe and Marion Blumpkist. They named her Jillian Anita.

The Blumpkists were a typical, blue collar family. The

father, a mechanic at a farm implement dealership, and the mother, a pharmacy tech for a small business owner. Jillian went to public school and attended a local junior college. She worked in various local department stores, call centers, and as a bank teller. In 1999, her parents were killed when a drunk driver crossed the center line of a two lane country road. She inherited a little bit of money, amount unknown, and left Minnesota.

"Jillian left here with some money and no ties at the age of thirty," Lainey said aloud. "Let's see what adventures or troubles she found."

She looked through the second and third set of papers and was frustrated to find that the pages behind the cover sheet had very little information that wasn't blacked out. Jillian had lived in Colorado, Utah, Texas, and Mexico before moving back to Minnesota last year. The only information on her activity during that time was a small entry that stated she had a relationship in Mexico with someone named Ru Fong.

She closed the file and raised her arms to stretch and yawn. She gently put the cat down from his comfortable spot on her lap. He meowed in disgust at being disturbed. "Sorry, Powie, time for bed. Helvig will have to wait till morning."

Lainey woke up most mornings around 4 a.m. Her usual routine was to start the Keurig, plug in a yoga video, shower, then turn on her computer. This morning, eager to get started with her research on Helvig, she skipped the exercise, filled her mega-sized coffee cup, and went straight to her computer.

She logged in and opened her favorite resource folder named Backgrounds. The small icon contained resource links her company used regularly while investigating a case. Each link had a dual security check-in with long, complicated passwords. The IT department was constantly reminding users about phishing emails, trojan horse emails that send worms through the entire server, and spam emails asking for money or alerts that a bank account had been compromised.

After an hour of searching the names of Herman Helvig, Brooks Olsen, and Jillian Blumpkist, and finding only their dates of births, she called her company's senior research guru, Snoops.

It was rumored that Clyde Bedlow could search something as large as Yellowstone National Park and find a tiny strand of fuzzy hair on a bowlegged mosquito. His genius had earned him the nickname of Snoops years ago.

"Hello, Lainey! How's it going in the frozen north territory called Minnesota?" Snoops asked.

"I said you could move up here with me, but you wanted to stay in our great state of Texas," she chuckled.

"Nope. I go to Canada ice fishing once a year and that's all the winter this southern boy can stand thank you very much!"

"Snoops, I'm working on a possible murder…"

"The Helvig case, right?" He interrupted. "Did you forget that I can trace everywhere you go on our server?"

"No, sir, I never forget that someone is watching when I'm logged in," she frowned. "I went through all the cyber security modules you sent me a few weeks ago."

She heard him snort and clear his throat before he spoke again.

"It's my job. Don't throw a hissy-fit this morning. I'm only trying to help you."

"I know, I know,"Lainey sighed. "What can you find on the Helvigs?"

Snoops was silent for a couple of moments and she could hear him typing away on his keyboard.

"Neither of them have any criminal records I can find

quickly, just the marriage records for Helvig and his wife." He paused, then continued. "When I can find only limited, general information on a person, it raises a red flag in my mind."

"I thought the same thing. I searched incognito mode in Google and still came up with very little information."

"I'm going to need to go beyond the Surface web, Lainey, and it may take a while to get back to you."

"I thought Google's incognito mode got me into the deep web on our server."

Snoops laughed. "No, incognito mode or private mode is simply an internet browser that keeps your browsing history from being stored. Incognito mode forgets or doesn't store the information once you close the browser. Field agents do not have access to the deep or dark web. Those searches have to come through me or my department for security reasons."

"I get confused sometimes trying to remember the difference in the deep web and the dark web," Lainey replied, opening her iPad. It was extremely rare that Snoops would divulge any tidbit of information about these sites, and she wanted to take notes just in case.

"Really expect me to buy that line?" He answered as if he was insulted. "I'm sending you the web training video we use for new hires."

"I'm sorry, Clyde. I didn't mean to anger you." She had learned a long time ago that if you get on the wrong side of Snoops, you better apologize using his real name asap. And she was hoping he didn't hang up on her.

"The training video is cued on your learning resources page. I expect you to get a perfect score on the attached test, too."

Poop! That boring video took an hour to watch!

"I will, I promise. Will you please work your magic and

find out information on the Helvigs and Jillian Blumpkist? *Please?*" she pleaded.

"It's not like you to beat around the bush trying to squeeze information out of me. Why now? Are you in over your head with the case?"

"Of course not!" Lainey forcefully stated. "I'm just frustrated." She paused and her voiced cracked. "And it's beginning to hit home that I'm not two doors down from your office. I miss everyone."

"We miss you, too," he said in a softer tone. "I'll start the process and put it as a rush in the whiteboard meeting this afternoon."

"Thank you. Tell everyone hello for me, okay?"

"You bet."

"Will you have something tomorrow?"

"I'll try. No promises."

"It was good to talk to you, Snoops."

"Yes, it was. But you still have to go through the training module again and pass the test."

"Okay, okay. I'll do it today," she grumbled and hung up.

Let's get this over with or he's going to call me on it.

She clicked on the learning resources link on her home page, found the module Snoops had added, and clicked start. She had taken all the training courses and remembered how hard the tests had been. These modules were designed so that if a person didn't listen and take notes, that person would not pass the test. She decided to use a yellow legal pad for notes instead of her iPad.

"Seems like I remember more if I write things down," she mumbled to the computer screen as the video began. "Here we go."

The module took more than an hour and when the video concluded, Lainey stood up to stretch, glancing down at the numerous pages of notes she had taken.

Typing on a computer all day has ruined my handwriting. For Pete's sake, I can barely read it.

She sat back down, took the notes to study before taking the dreaded test, and came up with a brief cheat sheet outline.

1. Surface web: sometimes called the 'clear net'

a. anything that can be found using various typical search engines like Bing, Safari, Google, etc.

2. Deep web: sometimes called the 'invisible web'

a. information that can't be found by typical search engines, examples are government databases, college libraries, medical or legal records, scientific knowledge. Nothing really illegal here. (Except hackers)

3. Dark web: very small part of the deep web that is intentionally hidden

a. consists of mostly illegal information, products, and services; only accessible through a browser or onion network that was first designed by the US Navy.

4. Other notes: It is almost impossible to trace personal information that is hidden deep within the dark web.

a. Illegal users: Terrorists, drug dealers, smugglers, and assassins. Some dark web illegal online stores are set up to resemble eBay or Amazon.

b. There are legal reasons to do online business for the degree of anonymity it provides. Examples include governments, law enforcement, journalists use it to contact sources, political bloggers, whistleblowers whose lives are in danger because of sensitive information they have.

c. Most activity is illegal in this area.

She read through the outline once more, then took the test.

Man, I missed one! Wonder if Snoops will know?

Lainey spent the next several hours responding to work emails and putting documentation into the proper programs.

"It takes more time to document everything than it does to investigate the actual case," she said to Powie, who was sleeping in the plastic inbox file beside her computer. As she shut down the computer, her cell phone rang. Usually if she didn't recognize the phone number, she would let it go to voice mail. Since she was new to the Mirror Falls and it was a local area code, she answered.

"Good afternoon. This is Lainey."

"Well, thank goodness this is your number! Francy looked it up for me, but I just don't trust those internet phonebooks. Give me the good old yellow pages anytime," the female voice said quickly. "This is Vera Abernathy, from church? You remember?"

"Yes, I remember you, Vera. How did you say you got my cell number?"

"Oh, Francy looked it up for me. She's a police dispatcher, you know."

"What can I do for you?"

"I've made dark chocolate chip mint bars for you. Can I bring them over now?"

Lainey looked around her small apartment. She still had boxes to unpack and the place was a bit messy to have company come over.

"That is very kind of you, Vera, but I'm still unpacking and haven't had a chance to get organized."

"Why didn't you say so? We will come right over and help you. Francy gets off soon. I'll call Della. See you in a short while!"

Vera hung up without giving Lainey a chance to respond. Within twenty minutes, the three ladies were at her front door. And they were carrying food.

"We're here!" Vera announced in her sing-song tone. "Hope you're hungry."

Lainey watched with surprise as the ladies came inside,

stopped in the entryway long enough to take off their shoes, and headed for the kitchen. The amount of food they brought would have fed an army.

"My goodness, I didn't expect you to bring a meal with you," Lainey said, the aroma of freshly baked bread filling the air.

"Mom says the best way to get acquainted is when your tummy is full," Francy smiled. "And when mom says to bring food, we bring food."

Lainey grinned.

"Isn't anybody going to introduce us? I'm Della Kristiansen. Vera tells me you're going to join our little Whoopee group."

"It's very nice to meet you," Lainey said, putting out her hand to shake Della's. Instead, the tall, well-dressed woman gave her a big hug.

"We hug around here," Della smiled.

"That's right," Vera chimed in. "You just never know where a person's hands have been!"

They all laughed.

"The food smells heavenly," Lainey said, sniffing the air. "How did you have time to make a turkey dinner with fresh bread?"

"I cheated a little bit," Vera grinned, looking over at Francy.

"She stopped at Breads by Betty and got a fresh loaf," her daughter replied. "And the baked turkey with all the fixings came from Coborn's Grocery."

"Stop telling all my secrets!" Vera commanded. "I did make the bars, you know."

"I appreciate this, Vera, and I can't wait to taste your bars. Maybe we should have dessert first." Lainey suggested.

Vera smiled. "You have to eat your meal first, young lady. The bars are for after we get you unpacked."

"Vera tells us that all the time. Eat first, then play cards, then treats," Della sighed.

Francy rolled her eyes and said, "Growing up, it was work first, then eat everything on your plate, work some more, then you could have a treat. My older brother, Jack, would sneak two or three cookies, bars, or whatever dessert mom had made, into his jeans pockets to eat later."

Vera smiled. "I figured that out one day when his laundry came out of the washer with chocolate stains all over them." Her lip quivered and her voice cracked as she was talking.

"We lost Jack several years ago," Francy said, giving Vera a hug.

"I'm so sorry for your loss," Lainey said. "The good memories don't erase the pain you feel from missing them."

Vera nodded, wiping away tears from her eyes.

"I lost Charlie seven years ago," Della reflected. "There are still days where all I do is cry."

A somber silence engulfed the group, and Vera was the first to speak again.

"Those boxes aren't emptying themselves while we sit here," she said. "And I don't want to wait forever to eat my bar!"

Francy patted her on the back. "You're right. Let's get busy."

"Where do you want us to start?" Della asked Lainey.

"There are only a couple of boxes left in the spare bedroom, one or two with towels, sheets, and bathroom items. Those in the front room are books and videos that go into the bookshelves."

"I'll take the bathroom duty," Della chuckled. "For some reason, I love to clean."

"I can do the spare bedroom," Francy said.

"I can put up books and videos. Maybe you have some I want to borrow." Vera suggested.

Lainey smiled, wondering if the ladies were really helping in order to snoop into her belongings. "I'll clean up the dinner dishes and the kitchen. If anyone has a question where something goes, just ask."

The ladies worked quickly and within an hour, they were finished.

"I'm ready for coffee and my bar," Vera announced. "Can you put on a pot?"

"I have a Keurig that makes a cup at a time," Lainey replied. "I have southern roasted pecan and regular flavor. Which would you like?"

"Decaf regular if you have it," Vera said.

"Ooh, southern roasted pecan sounds good," Della said, rubbing her hands together. "Dark chocolate chip mint and pecan coffee will hit the spot."

"I'm not a big coffee drinker," Francy stated, watching Vera roll her eyes. "Got a bottle of water?"

"Coming right up!" Lainey said.

"I can't understand why she doesn't like coffee," Vera commented, shrugging her shoulders. "I always had a pot brewing back in the day. It's not like she wasn't exposed to it."

"You make it sound like a crime or something to not like coffee," Francy grumbled. It was obviously a topic she and Vera had discussed many times.

Lainey filled their coffee cups while Vera cut her bars. They sat around the table, talking about the weather, chocolate, and generalities.

"Tell me more about the play we are going to see. Did you say it was at Brooksey's Playhouse?" Lainey asked, trying to gather more information. She still wondered if one or all of them might be involved in the Helvig case.

"I'm glad you reminded me," Vera said. "I've got a ticket for you in my purse."

"Thursday is closing night for the play Harold's Fantastic Cow. The story's about a farm boy raising a cow and going to an FFA show. I think it was written by a local high school teacher." Della stated, popping in her mouth the last bit of her bar.

"I've heard it is funny and sad," Francy said.

"Speaking of sad, wasn't it terrible about poor Brooksey? I can't believe she's gone. Such a lovely lady," Vera sighed, shaking her head in disbelief.

"Who knew she was a drug addict?" Della stated. "She was the sweetest person. Paul arranged the funeral for her."

"Who is Paul?" Lainey asked, wishing she could jot down a few notes.

"He's our mortician," Vera said. "And Della's second husband."

"Funeral Director is the preferred title," Francy scolded Vera, "I've told you that."

"In my day it was mortician." Vera stated stubbornly. "And don't correct your mother!"

It was Francy's turn to roll her eyes, which only maddened Vera.

"Don't you roll those big brown eyes at me," Vera cautioned, "I still have your dad's belt, you know."

Della grinned and patted Vera's hand. "He's been called a lot of things, so don't you worry about it."

Vera nodded in agreement.

"Paul and I married last year," Della continued. "He's a wonderful man, even if he does work with boring, dead people. They don't talk much," she laughed. "And he never asks to bring them home for dinner."

Lainey laughed. "I suppose you do need some sense of humor serving in that profession."

"Boy, that's the truth," Della replied.

"When you say your husband arranged the funeral, do

you mean it was held at his funeral home?" Lainey questioned.

"Paul has known the Helvigs for years. He did everything from preparing her body to hosting the funeral service."

"I've seen many drug addicts come through the jail," Francy added. "Sometimes they are hyped up, eyes bulging, angry, and difficult to handle. Others look perfectly normal. Brooksey must have known how to hide her addiction."

"Vera mentioned you're a dispatcher," Lainey said. "Do you work at the jail?"

"The jail is part of the police station," Francy replied. "I sit at the front desk, monitoring who comes in and out."

"How long have you been in law enforcement?"

"Gosh, it's been twenty years or so. Bet I've seen a thousand prisoners come and go during that time."

"Weren't you working when Brooksey was found?" Della asked.

"I wasn't. I heard it on my scanner at home."

"Did the police complete an investigation?" Lainey asked. By the look on Francy's face, she was afraid she might have questioned her a little too much.

"Yes, why?" Francy asked bluntly, staring at Lainey.

"I'm sorry if I sounded like I was interrogating you," she said trying to smooth things over. "Sometimes the investigator in me comes out before I think. I was just curious."

I'm not ready to tell them I'm working on the case. I need to know them better before I say anything.

"I loved Inspector Clouseau. He was funny, smart, and I think he finally caught the Pink Panther," Vera said.

"You still watch the British detective shows?" Della asked.

"Yes, I do. Jane Marple can solve anything!"

Everyone chuckled.

Francy looked at her watch. "We better head out. We've taken up Lainey's entire evening."

"It's not a bother," Lainey replied. "I've enjoyed having company and someone to talk with."

"We'll see you at Babe's Thursday at 5:15 p.m.," Vera said as they were leaving. "I think you'll enjoy our little theater group."

Lainey thanked them once more for the food and company, watching from the front door as they drove off.

"Well, that was an interesting evening," she said aloud as she closed the door. After putting food in the cat's dish, she turned off the lights and readied for bed. She noticed Francy had broken down the empty boxes and laid them in a stack on the floor in the spare bedroom. Della had meticulously put away the towels, arranging them by color and size, put a brand new toothbrush in the holder, and cleaned the mirror above the sink. It almost sparkled.

At least I know that Della and Francy pay attention to detail. Now, if only I can find my shampoo...

CHAPTER 4

Lainey was awakened by a loud crash and the sound of glass breaking. She glanced at the clock, rubbed her eyes, and checked to see if Powie was on the bed. The cat was nowhere to be found.

"It's 2:30 in the morning. You'd better not be climbing on the cabinets again, Powie," she said loudly as she headed toward the kitchen. She turned on the light expecting to see a broken water glass on the floor. Instead, she saw Powie, his eyes fixed on the back door, his tail fluffed out like he was about to pounce on something, meowing loudly.

Her gaze turned to the kitchen table that was sitting in front of the sliding patio door. It was covered with broken glass shards. The side of the glass door that opened onto the patio was shattered. She grabbed Powie, put him in the bedroom and shut the door behind her. She didn't want him stepping on any glass fragments. And, if someone was in the apartment, a locked door might buy her some time. She opened her nightstand drawer, took out the pistol she kept loaded, grabbed her cell phone, and dialed 911.

"This is 911. What is your emergency?"

"I've had a break-in and I'm not sure if someone is here or not. They broke the sliding door to the backyard. My address is..." Lainey began when she was cut off.

"Lainey? Is that you? This is Francy. I'm sending someone out immediately. Are you in a safe place?"

"I'm in the bedroom with the door locked. I have a pistol."

"I have a unit two streets west of your apartment. Tell me when you hear the sirens."

Lainey nodded, not realizing Francy couldn't see her.

"Did you hear me? Are you safe? Do you hear the sirens? Please respond," Francy said calmly, but forcefully.

"Yes, I'm safe." Her eyes were fixed on the doorknob, hoping to not see it twist or turn. "I do hear the sirens."

"Good. An officer will go around to the back and one to the front. Tell me when you hear their voices."

Lainey had been in tough situations before, but her heart was beating rapidly, and she knew her hand holding the gun was shaking.

Within a few minutes, she heard someone knocking on her bedroom window.

"Police! Are you able to open the window?" An officer shouted.

"Yes," she shouted as she hurried to open the large, floor length window. The officer came in, gun pulled, and quietly asked her to step away from the window.

"We are searching the perimeter. I'm going to open the bedroom door. Wait here till I tell you it's clear. Lock the door after me."

Lainey nodded and steadied her hand, still prepared to fire.

It wasn't long before the officer came back. He knocked before he opened the bedroom door.

"It's Captain Benson. Unlock the door and put away your weapon."

She lowered her gun and unlocked the door.

"I didn't find anyone hiding inside. Do you have an attic or hidden storage area?"

"No, I don't think so."

Benson's radio buzzed. "There is no one outside, Captain."

"Roger that."

Suddenly Lainey realized that she was still on the phone with Francy, who was now talking rather loudly to get someone's attention.

"Sorry, Francy, everything is okay," Lainey answered.

"I heard the radio conversation. Glad you are okay."

Captain Benson motioned for Lainey to hand him the cell phone.

"10-24 Dispatch. We will be 10-8. Copy?"

"10-4."

He hung up the phone and handed it back to Lainey.

"I need a statement from you about what happened," Benson said. "Can you do that now?"

Lainey told him she'd been asleep, heard glass breaking and thought her cat had broken a drinking glass. He smiled and said, "My wife has three cats. They can get into mischief."

She finished the story and asked him what was found outside.

"It looks like the glass was broken by shots from a pellet or BB gun. There were no other signs of break in."

He looked at Lainey. "You're new to Mirror Falls. How do you know Francy Baines?"

"I just met her a couple of days ago. She and her mom were here earlier this evening. They brought me supper and helped me unpack."

The captain grinned. "The Whoopee group must like you. Do you have something that could cover the back door for the night?"

"Yes, I have cardboard boxes and trash bags." Lainey quickly gathered the empty moving boxes from the spare bedroom, trash bags from under the kitchen sink, and a roll of duct tape. She began sweeping up the glass fragments while the two officers covered the opening in the back door.

"I think this will be secure for tonight. A patrolman will drive by your apartment a few times until morning. Call 911 if you need anything," the captain said, walking toward the front door.

Lainey thanked both officers and made sure the front door was locked after they left. Instantly, her cell phone started ringing.

"Hello?" Lainey answered.

"Are you okay? Do you want one of us to sleep over, so you are not alone?" Francy asked.

"No, no, I'm fine. What are you doing back at work?"

"I was called in for a half shift. My counterpart's wife went into labor and I guess he wanted to be there."

Lainey chuckled. "That would be my guess too."

"We've got large plastic tarps in the garage. I can bring one by to cover that back door."

"Thanks, but the officers taped up cardboard boxes and trash bags over the broken side. It'll be okay until I can call someone to replace it in the morning."

"Okay, then. Call me if you need anything. You have my cell number."

"Will do."

She looked at the collage of black garbage bags and flattened cardboard boxes covering most of the back door and sighed. Her cat had ventured out of the bedroom and was purring loudly.

"It's been a memorable few days in Mirror Falls, Powie," Lainey said as she bent down to pick him up. "Looks like we'll be camping in the front room tonight."

She took the comforter and blanket off her bed, grabbed her pillow and made a pallet next to her television. "I wish I had a sofa-sleeper," she said to Powie, who had already curled up at one end of the make-shift bed. She turned off the lights, turned on the night-lite app on her cell phone, and tried to fall asleep. The words her dad told her years ago when she became an investigator kept running through her mind.

If there is trouble, I won't be there to protect you. Promise me you'll sleep with one eye open.

"I'm doing that, Dad," she said softly.

Lainey woke up much later than usual. She stood up, rubbed the back of her neck, and turned on the television in time to catch the last local weather report before the national news started.

"Man, I have a crick in my neck this morning," she said aloud. She added water to the Keurig and was inserting the coffee pod when her cell phone rang. It was Snoops.

He's starting early. Maybe he has some interesting facts for me.

"Hey, Snoops. Kinda early for you to be at work, isn't it?"

"Very funny. Have you forgotten the 'bring-donuts-on-your-birthday' rule?"

Lainey laughed. "Well, happy birthday my friend! Did you send my maple-glazed donuts by FedEx or UPS?"

"Don't hold your breath," Snoops chuckled briefly. Then his tone turned more serious. "I pulled the information we had on the Helvig case and did several deep searches. Are you sure you don't have any other things to share with me? Remember, this is an official call and will be recorded."

"I don't think so," she replied a bit startled.

Why is he warning me to be careful about what I say?

"What did you find?" she asked him cautiously.

"Did you setup the interoffice internet phone we sent you?"

"Yes, I believe it's working."

"Call me on it as soon as possible."

"Yes, sir."

He hung up abruptly. Lainey looked around for the small, toy-like phone that she was issued.

"I'm not sure where I put the darn thing," she mumbled to herself, hurrying to find her iPad to take notes. She couldn't recall ever using this secure line when she worked in the office. Why now? What in the world did he find out?

She logged into the system, going through the many layers of security checks, and punched in the multi-digit code for Snoops. He answered on the first ring.

"Please put your cell phone in a closet or drawer in the room farthest from you." Snoops began. "Put me on hold till you return."

Now she definitely was concerned. She knew the reason for requesting a cell phone to be placed out of voice range was to prevent an outside source from monitoring or stealing information.

He thinks my cell phone is bugged!

She did as he asked, then returned to the secure line.

"It's done."

"Good," Snoops said. "Have you spoken with or interviewed Herman Helvig?"

"I spoke with him Monday evening."

"Where?"

Lainey paused. "It was at Brooksey's Playhouse downtown. That's where they found his wife, Brooks." She paused, took a deep breath and continued, "There was a hidden room several stories underneath the theater."

"A drug room," Snoops replied confidently.

"How did you know that?"

She could hear him take a big gulp of something and figured it was his morning coffee.

"It's a Meth lab most likely," he said after clearing his throat. "I found quite a bit about that building. Got your notepad ready?"

"I found an old newspaper article on the internet that said it had something to do with gangsters and human trafficking," she stated as she sat down, ready to take notes.

"I have many more hours of research on this case, but let's start with what information I have about Miss Ai Jiao Ju, alias Miss A."

For the next half hour, Snoops laid out the family tree of Miss A. She was born into a rich and powerful Chinese drug smuggling family in 1909. She had a daughter around 1933. It was not known when she came to America. The Stallion Saloon was opened in approximately 1942 and was used as a front for her family's drug and human trafficking purposes.

"Lainey, it appears the scope of this family's power covers several countries. I was unable to trace their activity when I first tried. There are many proxy networks and traps using botnets that can temporarily disable websites. I need more time and manpower to go further."

"Wow," she said. "Why do you think my cell phone might be bugged?"

"The extent of the protection in the Dark web for any information on this Miss A's family background is a red flag. My main goal is to make sure you are safe," he said. "You were in that building and shown the underground hideout or room. A bug or listening device could have been planted without your knowledge. Better safe than sorry."

She was speechless for a moment. When she regained her composure, she said hesitantly, "Thank you."

Sensing she was hiding something, Snoops probed a bit

further. "Has something else happened? This is serious, Lainey. Tell me."

"Last night the glass on my sliding back door was shattered from the outside. The police think shots from a pellet or BB gun caused the damage. No one was found inside or outside. It could have been kids."

She heard a loud sigh.

"Request that the police drive by your home several times during the coming nights. Tell them you will feel safer."

"That's a bit over the top, isn't it?" she asked.

"Until I can get accurate information on this case, my job is to make sure you are safe. Call them."

She agreed reluctantly.

"Use this line when you call me until I tell you otherwise. Let's follow procedure on this one, Lainey."

"Yes, sir."

"We will plan on talking in a few days. In the meantime, watch your step."

"Will do."

After hanging up the phone, she stared at the iPad notes, trying to absorb all she had just been told. Slowly, she stood up, put her iPad on her desk, and walked to the kitchen. She was still tired from last night's excitement and a bit concerned with Snoops' information.

"I need coffee," she said aloud as she looked again at the wall of black trash bags covering her door. "Think I'll reactivate my ADT home security system after I call the glass company."

By the end of the day, the glass had been replaced and the home alarm system installer was putting his tools away.

"I've tested each zone and they are working properly," the alarm installer said. "Most of the systems I work on are in the cities. I bet you're one of the most protected homes in Mirror Falls."

"Not many homes around here have security systems?" she asked.

"Mostly businesses like the bank and hospital. My family has lived on a farm west of town for years. We either know or are related to most of the town," he grinned. "We don't need to lock our doors."

Lainey's mind began churning with ideas and questions.

"Did you ever see a play at Brooksey's Playhouse?"

The man paused and stared at her for a few seconds, then dropped his gaze long enough to retrieve an electronic iPad from his tool belt.

"I have some paperwork for you to sign," he said coldly. The friendly tone in his voice was replaced with a guarded, almost monotone sound.

That struck a nerve! Why?

"You seem upset by my question. I apologize. I'm going to the Playhouse tomorrow and wondered what you thought of the theater," she said, keeping a close eye on his reaction.

He didn't respond and handed her the iPad to sign. Usually she would sign on the line and say goodbye. Suddenly, she felt the need to buy some time so she could ask more questions. She began reading the entire guarantee contract.

"It's the standard agreement," he said gruffly, obviously in a hurry to leave.

Lainey looked at the tiny, faded name that was embroidered on his shirt. She thought it said Mackie.

"Is Mackie a nickname?" she asked, still reading through the fine print.

"It's Maxie," he said bluntly, "it's a family name."

"Will you email me a copy of this, Maxie?" she said, hoping he would sign his last name on the iPad.

"It's emailed automatically."

"Okay. I'll watch my inbox."

The man nodded, opened the front door, and walked outside. Lainey grabbed the screen door to keep it from slamming shut.

"Thank you," she said loudly as he was getting into his van. She stood on the porch step smiling.

The man hastily backed out of the driveway, revving the engine. She heard his tires squeal as he drove away.

She walked back inside and called ADT.

Let's find out who you really are, Maxie.

"Hello, this is ADT. Would you like to schedule an appointment?"

"This is Lainey Maynard. My system was just installed by a wonderful man and I'd like to leave a good reference for him."

"We appreciate that. I will send you an email link to a survey where you can rate his service."

"That would be nice," she said. "I only saw his first name, Maxie, and want to make sure I give credit to the right person. Do you know his last name?"

"His name is Max Payton."

"Could you spell that please?"

"P-a-y-t-o-n," the female voice said.

"Thank you for your help. I'll look for your survey."

Lainey hung up and went to her work computer. She wrote Max Payton's name on a neon pink sticky note and stuck it on the screen.

"Well, Maxie," she said aloud as she turned on her wireless keyboard. "What are you hiding?"

She tried a general Google search, realizing quickly that without a middle name or birthdate, it would take too much time to look through the hundreds of results. She searched for Mirror Fall's local newspaper, *The Midwest Echo*. When the home page loaded, she clicked on the story archives link.

"Max Payton," she typed in the tiny article search box. She tapped her finger on her chin as she waited for the results. "Either this is a very slow connection or dear Maxie has a lot of references," she muttered impatiently, looking down at Powie sitting beside her chair. Finally, a few articles appeared, and Lainey anxiously read through them, clicking on the one titled "Local Farm Boy Gets Full Ride AG Scholarship".

If Maxie had a scholarship to the University of Minnesota twenty years ago, why is he now an installer for ADT?

Before she could search further, the doorbell rang, followed by very loud knocking.

Lainey, still cautious from the previous night's uninvited guest, peeked out the window of her office to see who it was. To her surprise, it was Vera, Francy and Della.

"I'm coming," she shouted as she hurried to unlock the door.

"Honey, when I heard what happened last night, I told the girls we were coming over to make sure you were okay," Vera exclaimed as she rushed through the doorway. Francy and Della were close behind.

"I'm really fine. You didn't need to…"

Vera hugged her with such force, she thought she might fall backward.

"Oh, no you're not," Francy said, taking her turn to give a bear hug. "The captain filled me in. He said you were very brave but shaken up."

"I haven't lived here long," Della said as she hugged her, too. "This town may be small, but it can be difficult to fit in."

"Unless you have relatives around here," Vera added. "Then, you are in like Flynn."

"Mom, you watch too many of those old Errol Flynn movies," Francy said, shaking her head.

"I happen to love those black and white movies," Vera said proudly.

"I do appreciate your concern," Lainey replied, trying not to chuckle. "The door has been replaced and I reconnected my ADT security system." She watched as Della and Francy walked over to exam the new glass in the back door.

"Did Arnie do the door installation?" Della asked as she opened and closed the glass door. "He's my neighbor and is the best glass man around."

"Yes," Lainey said, nodding in agreement. "He was very gracious to work me in today."

"I've known Arnie for years and years," Vera said. "But you have to watch Annie."

"Annie is his wife," Della replied, winking at Francy. "Vera thinks she cheats at cards."

"Think? I know she does! They would come to our house on Friday nights to play Hearts. Doc always said that gal would cheat in front of her own mother!"

Laughter filled the room. For the first time since moving to Mirror Falls, Lainey felt comfortable.

"We hope you'll still come to the Playhouse with us," Francy said.

"I wouldn't miss it for the world," she found herself saying.

They seem sincere. Do I really know them enough to trust them?

"Now that's settled, let's play Farkle," Vera said, taking a sandwich bag of red dice out of her purse. "I'm not that good at dice games, so this is your chance to beat me… just this once," she grinned.

The ladies left around 9 p.m. As Lainey waved goodbye and locked the front door, she realized how much she enjoyed the evening.

"These are special ladies," she thought to herself. "I think I'm going to like being in the group."

Checking the back door twice, she turned on the alarm system, and got ready for bed.

"Come on, Powie," she said, picking him up. "I think we will both sleep better tonight."

CHAPTER 5

It had been a quiet night and Lainey's purring alarm cat woke her as usual at 4 a.m. She had slept soundly and felt confident she could tackle whatever the day brought her way. But first, she needed coffee.

As she walked into the kitchen, she turned off the security alarm that had been installed in the utility room just inside the doorway. She heated up the coffee maker and glanced at the sliding glass back door. She was relieved it was still intact.

There was a sticky note on her fridge that read *buy coffee goop*. She had completely forgotten about being out of her favorite almond flavored coffee creamer.

Years before her dad died, he had tried to get her to like the taste of plain coffee. He said all the goop she put in it was going to clog her arteries. From that time on, she always asked for coffee goop, mostly to get a rise out of him.

"Wonder if there is a drive thru place to get coffee this early in the morning?" She said aloud as she grabbed her cell phone. She hit the Google search box microphone and said, "Nearest Starbucks." She was surprised to see that the nearest

Starbucks was some fifty miles away. Instead, the name Caribou Coffee was listed, and it was less than two miles away.

Still in her house shoes and pj's, she got in her car and followed the GPS directions to the shop. The drive thru lane was open. She drove up and was reading their menu when a cheery voice came over the speaker.

"Good morning. You're new in town, aren't you?"

Lainey stopped reading and looked around the ordering menu sign to see if someone were standing outside the building.

"Hello? What can I get you to drink?" the voice prompted.

"Uhm, hello," Lainey said carefully. "Why do you ask if I'm new in town?"

"Our drive thru has a video camera," the voice said. "And I didn't recognize your car."

Lainey was silent, still trying to find the camera.

"We have regulars that come at this time each day," the voice continued. "What can I get you?"

"A skinny mocha frappe with no whipped cream, please."

"Ma'am," the voice said politely, "Caribou Coffee's version of that is called a Northern Lite Mocha. Would you like milk chocolate or dark chocolate and what size this morning?"

"A small is fine and dark chocolate, please."

"Of course, and no whipped cream, correct?"

"Correct."

"I'll get your total at the next window. Please drive forward."

Lainey drove ahead, and a cute young girl wearing a black hairnet appeared, opening the window.

"That will be $5.78," she said, holding out her hand.

Lainey paid her and waited for the change.

"Here's your change and here's your coffee," the girl said, handing the change and the hot cup to her at the same time.

She took the change and put it in the middle console of her car. As she turned back to the window to grab her coffee, she didn't realize the young girl had leaned forward in order to stretch out her arm into the car window. Lainey's left arm bumped the girl's hand, spilling the coffee down the outside of her car and down the inside of her door. The girl looked down at the cup on the ground and then back at Lainey. Her nice smile turned into a deep frown.

"I'm sorry," Lainey said, "I didn't see your hand. Do you have extra napkins?"

The girl said nothing, closed the window and returned with a few napkins.

"We are making another one," she said curtly, watching Lainey trying to mop up the spilled coffee.

"Thank you. That would be great."

Within a minute, the young girl was back at the window with another cup of coffee.

"Here's your coffee. Do you want to come inside to pick it up?" the girl quipped.

"That's not necessary," Lainey replied as politely as possible. "I can hold on to it."

As she drove away, she looked in the rearview mirror and noticed that a line had formed in the drive thru lane.

If those are the regulars, I sure hope they don't spill their coffee.

She pulled into her garage and by 7:30 a.m., she had finished her coffee, showered, dressed, and was sitting in front of her computer. Her calendar was synced with all her devices and before starting work each day, she checked it just in case she had an appointment she had forgotten. Today the list included a few follow up calls, updating documentation files, and Brooksey's Playhouse.

She opened her email and saw a secure message from Snoops. She changed servers and then opened the file. Now that cyber criminals and hackers were common threats in the business world, she knew anytime she was logged on to the server, her movements, or clicks, as her IT guru called them, were being monitored. It made her uncomfortable.

"It's like I'm the hacker or something," she grumbled as she began reading. There was not a greeting from Snoops. No hello or good morning. The subject line had two words: Time Line.

As Lainey read, a familiar tingling sensation like goose bumps all over her arms began. She knew it was adrenaline so she made herself slow down, and keep focused.

Ai Jiao Ju - born 1909 - the only child of a powerful and affluent Chinese family with ties to human and drug trafficking. Groomed to be involved in the family business; apparently ran a prostitution operation using captive females. In 1932, relocated to United States to expand family's power and influence and possibly head a drug smuggling operation with Mexico. Started a brothel in small town of Mirror Falls, Minnesota, Miss A's Stallion Saloon, as a front for trafficking and to develop business relationships with various gangsters of the day. She gave birth to a girl, Li Jang, in late 1933. Still searching for birth father.

She continued to operate the brothel until late 1949 or early 1950. Found evidence of her returning to China in 1950, going to Mexico in 1953, and traveling back to the States sometime in 1955. A picture of a gravestone was uncovered in a search of old microfiche sheets. The name appears to be Ai Jiao. Date of death 1980. That has not been verified at present.

Li Jang - born 1933 - the only known child of Ai Jiao Ju. Not much information on her childhood although it appears she may have been raised in Mexico. According to hospital records in Minneapolis, she gave birth to a daughter, Annchi Bao, in 1955. No birth father given.

Annchi Bao - investigation in progress.

Lainey sat back in her chair trying to process the information she had just read when the interoffice internet phone rang. She knew it was Snoops.

"Is your cell in a safe, secure place?" he asked.

"Yes," she fibbed as it sat on her desk.

Instantly, her cell rang loudly. It stopped before she could turn it off.

"Take care of that now," Snoops said harshly.

She did as he instructed, knowing that she was going to be chewed up and spit out for lying when she returned.

"It has been put away, Clyde," she said sheepishly. "My apologies."

There was a long, awkward silence that was almost deafening. She dreaded the reprimand that was coming.

"A new cell phone will be delivered to you this afternoon. It has the contacts you frequently call, and your email is ready to go. Ship the old phone to me in the same box that the new one arrives in. I expect to have it tomorrow morning by 10 a.m."

"Thank you," she replied. "It will be in your office."

"Do you have any questions on the report?" He asked even though he knew she did.

"I sure do," she said, rather happy not to be chewed out. "Did I mention that I'm going back to Brooksey's Playhouse this evening?"

"You don't need to be meeting Helvig in that location again," he barked.

"Calm down. I'm not meeting Helvig. I'm going to a play tonight with a group of ladies."

She could hear him typing on his keyboard.

"Harold's Fantastic Cow," he mused. "I know you. What else are you planning on doing while you enjoy this captivating production?"

"I'm hoping that Jillian Blumpkist will be there," she said, smiling.

"I thought as much," he sighed. "These ladies wouldn't happen to be called the," he paused as if he were making sure he had the correct wording, "Whoopee group, would they?"

She was stunned for a minute, realizing that he knew more than he was sharing.

"Are you having me followed? Why? It takes all of three minutes to go from one end of Mirror Falls to the other." She questioned in an angry tone.

"We are not having you followed," he said quietly, trying to keep her quick temper at bay. "You should be thankful I'm watching out for you."

She paused to think before answering.

"You called the police station and spoke with Captain Benson, didn't you?"

"That would be the logical answer, wouldn't it?" He chuckled. "I wanted to see if you had requested the police to drive by your apartment as I told you to do."

She rolled her eyes and was glad the interoffice phone didn't have video attached to it.

"They seem like very sweet ladies," she said. "What information have you found on Jillian?"

"Nothing more than what you gave me."

"What do you have on Helvig? Brooksey? Or that Ru Fong fellow?" She sounded like a drill sergeant.

When she heard Snoops clearing his throat, she wondered if she had pushed him a bit too far.

"We have forty other agents in this organization, Lainey." He said in a low, controlled, monotone voice. "The information needs to be accurate and I'm getting it to you as quickly as possible."

"I realize how busy you are, and I appreciate your patience with me."

She could hear him sigh once more.

"We've worked together for a long time. I'm sure it's difficult for you to not be in the main office. Let's plan on talking again Saturday."

"Thanks, Snoops."

"If something urgent comes up or the situation around you changes, contact me asap."

"You know I will."

"And, Lainey, don't feel sorry for the cow if it is turned into hamburger by the end of the play."

She grinned. "I'll make sure you get the first six patties if that happens."

The rest of the day flew quickly by. When she finally looked up from her computer screen, it was after 4 p.m. She shut down her computer, changed her clothes, and touched up her hair.

"I hope it will be an enlightening evening, Powie. Guard the castle for me."

Lainey grabbed her purse and keys and paused, wondering if she should take the iPad with her. She was used to having it in the car. It had come in handy many times. She hesitated for only a second, picked up the device, turned on the alarm system, and opened the garage door.

She got in the car and noticed the lived-in look it had. The passenger seat held a roll of paper towels, a CD case filled with audio books, a little fabric bag for her iPad, and the scratch notepad she had gotten from the glass repair man. An umbrella, a purple exercise jacket, and a heavy coat lay on the floor mat in front of the passenger seat. There was an unopened, 24 pack of bottled water sitting on the floor behind her seat.

"Guess I do live in my car," she sighed as she adjusted the rearview mirror and backed out of the garage.

Lainey arrived twenty minutes ahead of the scheduled

meeting time. She wanted to look around Babe's House of Caffeine before the others arrived. As she got out of her car, she heard a loud honking behind her. She looked back to see Vera driving up beside her with the passenger window rolled down.

"I'm glad I caught you," Vera shouted. "Change of plans for supper. We're going to the Chinese Palace instead. It's only a jump and a skip away from here. Follow me."

Vera rolled up the window and drove away.

Lainey quickly got back in her car and tried to follow. Vera's car was already out of sight.

"Glad I have a GPS," she said aloud. "Siri, driving directions to the Chinese Palace Restaurant."

Siri answered in the British male voice she had programmed into her phone, "Chinese Palace is three minutes away. Travel two blocks and turn right after stopping." The sexy voice spouted the full directions and in no time she was at her destination.

The Chinese Palace was a block away from Brooksey's Playhouse. Lainey hadn't noticed it the night she met with Helvig. The three ladies were waiting for her in the parking lot.

"Whoop, whoop, whoop!" Della greeted Lainey. "Did you have a difficult time following Vera?" One corner of her mouth had turned upward in the slightest of grins.

Vera wrinkled her nose. "She didn't have trouble following me. My Buick may be old, but the taillights work just fine!"

"Let's go inside," Francy chuckled. "We don't want to be late for the play."

The restaurant's entrance was flanked by a pair of four foot tall golden Buddhas. An almost regal floor length curtain of shiny gold beads stood between the statues. The smell of incense and soy sauce floated in the air.

"Welcome to the Palace," a man's voice greeted as the beaded wall parted in the middle to let them pass.

"I never get tired of that greeting," Francy said. "The recording and the curtain opening must be triggered by sensors when you get close to the statues."

Lainey followed the others inside, expecting to see a typical Chinese buffet complete with people milling around several serving lines, soft drink stations, and a checkout counter. Instead, she felt instantly transported to an ancient palace waiting for a king to make his grand entrance.

Chinese folk music played softly in the background, complete with strings, flutes, and drums. There were pillars etched in gold leaf, shiny foil wallpaper, high ceilings with scenes of beautiful gardens and trees painted on them. Waitresses, wearing deep red kimonos trimmed with embroidered gold dragons seemed to float on air as they walked silently between guest tables. They were beautiful. The white makeup and large hairpins holding their hair in place added to their charm.

"It's a bit unexpected for a restaurant in Mirror Falls, isn't it?" Francy said, watching Lainey's expression.

"What do you think? Ever see this in Houston?" Della asked.

"To say I'm amazed is an understatement."

"Wait till you meet the manager," Francy said.

"I swear his eyes are the most brilliant shade of green I've ever seen," Vera sighed.

A waitress walked up to the group, bowed, and said, "Please, follow me to your table."

"Mom likes to sit in the back of the room," Francy whispered to Lainey.

She led them to a round table draped in a royal purple cloth with place settings formal enough for a dinner at the

White House. After they sat down, the waitress bowed, and walked silently away.

"I love coming here," Vera said as she smoothed out her cloth napkin. "It reminds me of the movie The King and I."

"Please don't start singing *Whistle a Happy Tune* again," Francy begged. "I've heard that a million times."

Della and Lainey looked at each other and laughed.

I certainly wasn't expecting to find an elegant place like this in Mirror Falls. Wonder how the owner can make a living in this small town?

"I thought this was a buffet," Lainey said, looking at the elaborate menu in front of her.

Francy, Della, and Vera looked at each other and grinned.

"You'll see," Della said softly.

Their waitress reappeared, bowed, and said, "We are ready to serve you."

Lainey watched as several waitress stood in a line, each carrying a different dish. Silently and efficiently, each waitress put a serving from their dish onto her plate: fried rice and white rice, egg rolls, several types of meat dishes with vegetables, fried shrimp, and cream cheese wontons.

"We can ask for sushi if you want," Francy said, watching Lainey's reactions to the parade of food being presented.

"This is amazing! I'm not a big sushi fan and I'm not sure I can finish what's on my plate now!"

"Thank heaven for that," Vera said, obviously relieved. "I wasn't going to say anything, but I don't like having raw fish on my plate. Might as well go to Charlie's Bait Stop and eat minnows."

"It's not minnows," Della replied, laughing.

Vera wrinkled her nose and shook her head. "Not for me. Now, let's eat."

As the ladies ate, Lainey listened, laughed, joined the conversation at times, and smiled.

It's been a long time since I've laughed so much. I like these ladies.

"I've been meaning to ask how you got the name Whoopee group?"

Francy smiled. "Della always greets us with *whoop, whoop, whoop*. Hence the name."

"She is always so cheery," Vera said, looking at Della.

"I'm the cheery funeral director's better half," Della giggled.

"We'd better finish and head over to Brooksey's if we want a good parking spot," Francy said.

"What about our checks?" Lainey asked.

"They have them at the checkout counter," Vera said as she stood up. "Follow me."

Instead of walking toward the front of the restaurant, Vera headed toward the back of the room turning right into a hallway adorned with the same lavish decor. At the end of the hallway was a small counter where another beautiful waitress was waiting.

"Good evening, Vera," the waitress said. "Was everything to your satisfaction?"

"It always is," Vera replied. "This is Lainey Maynard. It was her first time here."

The waitress nodded. "Welcome and we hope you will come again."

As they walked to their cars, Vera reminded them, "Let's try to park close to each other. It will be dark when we get out."

Lainey got in her car. She yawned, and filling the fullness in her stomach, gently pinched her cheeks. "Wake up Lainey. You've got to be alert at Brooksey's."

CHAPTER 6

There were no parking places open in front of the theater, but there were empty spaces in the rear parking lot. They got out of their cars and hurried inside. The entry was crowded with people standing in lines in front of the staircases, the ticket desk, and the main floor entrance. Everyone was talking at the same time creating a loud sound resembling the static heard between radio station channels. Lainey looked for Herman Helvig, but she couldn't see over the lines of people.

"Our seats are in the west balcony," Francy directed as she got in line. "Looks like a full house tonight."

The line moved quickly and when the lights dimmed, a voice announced it was time for guests to find their seats. The ladies walked up the stairs and to Lainey's surprise, their seats were in the front row of the center section.

Good. The balcony might make it easier to find Helvig.

She sat between Della and Francy. The lights were still on and people were still finding seats.

"Do either of you know the manager, Jillian Blumpkist?" Lainey questioned.

"I've seen her a few times," Della said, watching the people below. "She seems nice."

"Brooksey was friends with Mom," Francy said. "She was fond of Jillian."

"Is she here this evening?"

"I would think so," Della replied. "Normally she introduces the play and the cast at the end."

The lights darkened slowly as a spotlight appeared on the stage. A hush came over the crowd when the center curtain opened slightly. A woman walked into the spotlight and the crowd applauded. She bowed and waited for the applause to die down. Lainey leaned forward to get a closer look at Jillian.

"Welcome to our playhouse," she began. "My name is Jillian Blumpkist." She bowed slightly as the crowd applauded again. "We are glad you joined us for the last performance of Harold's Fantastic Cow. The cast and crew have worked very hard to bring you a glimpse into the life of a special boy named Harold and his most fantastic cow. There will be a short intermission between Acts II and III as listed in your program. Feel free to go to our food and beverage area during that time. Now, please turn off all cell phones and recording devices, sit back, and enjoy the show." The crowd applauded once more as she walked off the stage.

Lainey leaned over to Francy and whispered, "I'd like to meet Jillian after the play. Where is her office?"

"She'll be standing in the greeting line with the cast."

The orchestra began playing and Lainey found herself focusing on the almost invisible black door Helvig had shown her instead of the characters on the stage. She fidgeted through the first two acts, laughing when the crowd laughed and clapping when they clapped. When the lights came up for intermission, she quickly excused herself.

"I'd really like to talk with Jillian," she said to the ladies. "Don't worry if I'm a little bit late for the curtain call."

As she hurried to the stairway to beat the crowd, she felt a tug on her shoulder. It was Francy.

"Why are you so interested in Jillian?"

"No specific reason."

"Do you want to ask her about Brooksey?"

Lainey stopped and look directly at Francy.

What does she know?

"Why did you ask that?" she questioned.

Francy paused, looked at the people around her, then moved a little closer to Lainey.

"Let's walk to your car. Then we can talk."

The two made their way downstairs and stepped outside without drawing attention to themselves. They walked silently over to Lainey's car.

"What is the nature of your interest in Jillian Blumpkist," Francy said with a business-like tone in her voice. Her friendly smile had been replaced with a straight line.

Lainey studied the change in her face. She'd seen that look many times. She was being interrogated.

Be cautious here. You don't know her that well. Think before you speak!

"I realize we don't know each other very well," Lainey began, keeping her eyes directly on Francy's. "Since you work at the police station, I'm sure you are privy to information on cases that may not be made public."

Francy was now studying her facial expressions.

Trying to figure out if I'm lying, aren't you? You won't catch me that way.

"Let's cut to the chase," Francy stated frankly. "I know you are an investigator. Is your company investigating Brooks Helvig's death?"

"Is there an ongoing police investigation into her death?

Do they suspect it was murder?" Lainey questioned determinedly.

The two women stared at each other in silence, trying to decide whether to trust each other.

Finally, Francy broke the silence.

"Yes, there is an investigation concerning the death of Brooksey," Francy admitted. "And I'm taking a huge risk by telling you this."

Lainey nodded. "And you understand that I'm taking the same huge risk by telling you that my company has been asked to investigate a large life insurance claim."

"My gut tells me I can trust you," Francy said, relaxing a bit. Her smile was returning.

"Mine, too. Let's see if we can help each other out on this, okay?"

"Okay. Mind skipping the third act of the play?"

"I haven't been paying attention to it anyway," Lainey admitted. "We can go back inside before the play is over."

The two smiled at each other.

"Tell me what you can about the police investigation, and I'll share with you what I know."

"I want you to know upfront that I think we should talk with Captain Benson about anything we discuss between us."

"Agreed."

"There is some indication that Brooks' death may not have been accidental."

"I was beginning to suspect."

"No information is being shared with the public at this time and as far as I know, the public thinks it was an overdose and nothing more. But I do know our detective has been very busy following any and all leads. What does your company suspect?"

"There was a large life insurance policy taken out on

Brooks a short time before her death," Lainey said, pausing to consider whether to continue.

"And the beneficiary was Jillian, right?" Francy finished Lainey's thought.

"Yes. Herman Helvig called our company and asked us to investigate. I met with him earlier this week. He is not fond of Jillian and feels that she is somehow involved with his wife's death."

Francy crossed her arms and thought for a moment.

"That makes some sense," she began. "He's been almost too eager to point the finger at Jillian."

"Did your detective talk with him?"

"He talked to him a couple of times. First, the night Brooks' body was found, and then again at the station. He was not convinced that Helvig was telling the truth nor did he believe that Brooks was an addict. But so far, he hasn't found any evidence to prove Helvig lied."

"Did you know the Helvig's? Was Brooks the kind, caring philanthropist that I've heard she was?"

"Mom has known them for years. They used to come over and play canasta when dad was alive. She was exactly that, kind and patient. I can't think of one person in this town who didn't like her."

"What about Herman?"

"As a kid, I saw him laugh and drink beer with Dad, but he never had anything to do with me or my brother. He's a very shrewd businessman and if you're rich, he's the greatest thing since sliced bread. If you're not, you wouldn't be worthy enough to clean the mud off his boots. A real jerk, if you ask me."

Lainey nodded. "I read him as a chauvinist. He may dress to the nines, but his overly high regard for himself is evident. What do you know about Jillian?"

"She's been in town a couple of years now and I've

bumped into her a few times. This is a small town where everyone knows everything that goes on. Jillian has managed to stay off the local gossip radar."

"Let's go back inside before the play ends. I want to make sure I meet her."

They walked back into the theater as the main floor doors were being opened.

"Good timing," Francy said. "Let's wait for Mom and Della to come downstairs. Then we can head over to greet the actors."

"Where have you two been?" Vera asked as she walked up to Francy. "I may never eat hamburger meat again!"

"I had some business that needed my attention and Francy came to check on me."

They got in line to congratulate the actors. Jillian was on the end closest to the exit.

"Hello," Lainey said as she shook Jillian's hand. "I understand you are the manager. May I congratulate you on the production."

"Thank you. It was a group effort."

"I realize you are busy, but would you have time to speak with me briefly."

"Of course. If you can wait at the ticket counter, I will be finished in a moment."

Lainey said goodbye to the Whoopee group and walked over to the counter. Pretending to look at the posters and brochures, she noticed a small golden Buddha perched beside the computer screen. She glanced over to see that Jillian was still greeting guests before picking up the object. It had a grinning face and what looked like a green gemstone in the middle of its belly. She immediately thought of the jade globe on Helvig's desk.

Interesting. Wonder if it is jade.

She was startled by a voice behind her. "I see you are a fan of Buddha."

Lainey turned around quickly and saw the strikingly beautiful woman watching her carefully. Jillian had a flawless olive complexion and shiny black hair that hung gracefully down to her shoulders. Her piercing green eyes shimmered like diamonds in the sunlight.

"My apologizes," Lainey said as she handed her the statue. "I was admiring the gemstone."

"It is jade," Jillian said. "I like to think it guards my computer."

She walked behind the desk and returned the statue to its place.

"Would you like to audition for the next play?"

Lainey chuckled. "No, I'm not quite ready for prime time."

"How can I help you?"

I've got to ease into this. Don't want to alert her just yet.

"My name is Lainey Maynard. I recently moved to Mirror Falls for my work."

"I'm sure you'll find it a lovely town. Do you work in the Arts?"

"Not exactly. I'm an insurance investigator."

Lainey watched closely for any reaction from Jillian. There was none.

"I see. What can I help you with?"

"I'd like to ask you about Brooks Helvig."

"She was a wonderful person."

She is a cool cookie. Let's see just how long she can keep her cool.

"Do you have plans for the million dollars she left you?"

Jillian's eyes narrowed making her gaze even more penetrating. She stood up, walked out from behind the desk and stood directly in front of Lainey.

"Unfortunately, I do not have time to speak with you further this evening. Come here tomorrow at 10 a.m. Bring proof of who you say you are, your employer, and your interest in my personal affairs."

With that, Jillian nodded slightly and walked back into the main theater.

"I will see you tomorrow morning," Lainey called after her.

She left the Playhouse and was checking her phone messages while she walked to her car. There was a text from Francy requesting that she call when she arrived home. She noticed a man standing beside her car when she looked up. She stopped dead in her tracks.

"Ms. Maynard." The man began speaking without moving toward her. "I see I have frightened you. Rest assured I am not here to hurt you."

Lainey didn't move. She had her hand on her phone ready to push the panic button.

"My name is Ru Fong. I believe you have questions concerning Jillian?"

She said nothing, looking around for other people who might be close enough to help her.

"Even the night air has ears," he continued. "In the morning before your meeting with Jillian, come to the back entrance of the Chinese Palace. I will be there to meet you."

With that, he nodded, turned, and walked away, disappearing into the shadows of the rear parking lot. Hurrying to her car, she got in quickly, slammed the door and locked it. As she started the engine, she saw the fortune cookie taped to her steering wheel. She sped out of the parking lot and didn't relax until she was parked in her garage. She grabbed the cookie, got out of the car and hurried into her apartment, still feeling as if someone was behind her.

She turned on the alarm system and walked into the kitchen. It was several minutes before her heartbeat returned to a normal pace. Her first thought was to call the police station and report what happened. But nothing really happened. There was nothing to report. Almost as if on cue, her cell rang.

"Hello? This is Lainey."

"Sorry we couldn't talk further," Francy was saying. "Come to the station tomorrow. It's important we keep Captain Benson in the loop here. I can't afford to lose my job and maybe he has information that might help your investigation."

"Sure. I need to get to know the people at the station anyway. Will afternoon work?"

"I'll check with him and let you know the time."

"Thanks," Lainey replied. She ended the call and looked at the fortune cookie she'd put on the countertop. She picked it up and tore open the wrapper. It looked like a normal fortune cookie. There was nothing special or irregular about it. She cracked it open and took out the strip of paper inside. There was writing on one side and she read it over several times.

"Family ties run deep," she said aloud. She turned the strip of paper over and saw only a symbol, 五. Usually, the English translation was listed below, but not this time. She opened her iPad, took a picture of the symbol, and did a Google search for it. Hoping it was a number of some sort, she tried to narrow down results. Sure enough, she found a symbol that resembled the one in the cookie. It was for the number five.

One website showed the number five was associated with both good luck and bad luck, depending on how it was used. Another that it was connected to the five elements: water, fire, earth, wood, and metal. Still another site noted people with the lucky number five tend to search for freedom from their surroundings or other people.

Lainey put down the iPad, put the strip of paper in her purse, and yawned. She checked to see that the windows and doors were locked and checked again to make sure the alarm was turned on. She walked into the bedroom and saw her cat sound asleep at the foot of the bed.

"I'm tired, Powie," she said as she pulled back the covers, disrupting his snoring. He meowed weakly, stood up and sauntered over to her pillow. She stroked his back for a second. "Sometimes I wish you were a guard dog. I would take you with me tomorrow." She turned off the light and fell asleep.

CHAPTER 7

Lainey was up earlier than usual working in her office. She wrote notes, trying to recount specific details of the previous evening's happenings. She was glad to see that Snoops had emailed her more information and didn't request she do the same. She opened the email and grinned as she read the subject line *World of Helvig*. Her mood turned more solemn as she read through the text.

Herman Abe Helvig - born 1954 to Abe Helvig and Bertha (Winchell) Helvig. Father and Grandfather Helvig were in law enforcement, had an older sister who died from scarlet fever 1955. He attended a community college before taking a job at a local bank, Prime One. No evidence of a four-year degree. Criminal records show he was arrested several times for drunk and disorderly conduct, but no judgements handed down. Married Brooks Olsen in 1967 and had no children. Passport records indicate he travels frequently to China and Taiwan. Financial investigation is in progress.

Brooks Elizabeth Olsen - born 1955 to Sven and Sara Olsen, farmers until their deaths in 2008. She had several

older siblings, all deceased. Graduated from University of Northwestern, St. Paul, Minnesota. Accomplished pianist. No criminal records found. Founded the Mirror Falls Arts Society in 2012, responsible for starting Brooksey's Playhouse. Note: title shows the owner of the Playhouse is Arts For Mirror Falls, LLC. Herman Helvig is listed as CEO.

Ru Fong - born 1970. Names of parents are unknown. One sister born 1979. Graduated from the prestigious Le Cordon Bleu Culinary Institute, Shanghai, in 1992. Traveled back to Mexico City and worked for a restaurant chain until relocating to Minneapolis in 2013 to manage a large hotel restaurant. Moved to Mirror Falls in 2017 and currently manages the Chinese Palace.

Lainey sat back in her chair trying to digest what she had just read. She decided to print both emails Snoops sent her and take with her when she talked to Captain Benson. Her mind was racing with all sorts of connections between Helvig, Ru, and Jillian.

"Don't get ahead of yourself," she said aloud. She decided to meet with Ru Fong before talking to Jillian and it was time to leave. "Where did I pack my pocket voice recorder?"

She searched through her desk and found the tiny recording device. Even though more updated versions didn't require a small cassette to record on, she had always received clear recordings each time she used it. She changed the battery and slipped the device in her sweater pocket.

The clock on her microwave read 8:30 a.m. She put on her coat, set the security alarm, and got into her car. She felt her pocket once more just to double check the device was there. She pulled out of her driveway and had parked in the back of the restaurant by 8:45 a.m. She looked around the empty parking lot. Last evening, cars were fighting for a spot to park as close to the back door as possible. This morning, a single trash dumpster stood watch over the abandoned lot.

"Okay, Ru Fong," she said to herself as she looked in her rearview mirror. "I'm here. I hope you are ready for my questions."

She got out of her car and walked to the metal back door. There was no doorbell or video camera that she could see. She knocked forcefully, stepped back, and switched on her audio recorder. She heard several clicking sounds and the door opened. A petite young girl was holding the door open.

"Please, come in. Mr. Fong is waiting for you."

Lainey entered and noticed that this entrance was not elegantly decorated like the front of the restaurant. The walls were painted a very dark grey. No pictures, no gold leaf or foil wallpaper. Two oblong florescent light fixtures flickered as they worked hard to provide some light. She walked down the hallway toward what looked like a screen door.

"His office is to the left," the young girl said. She walked in front of her and opened the door.

Lainey walked through the door and heard it shut behind her. "Thank you," she said as she turned to talk to the young girl. But there was no one behind her. The girl hadn't followed her through the doorway.

She turned back around. Her eyes had to adjust to the brightness of the glaring white bare walls. She looked down a short hallway that had one door on the left just before it made a sharp turn to the right. She moved closer to the door, noticing there was no name plate on it.

Here goes nothing.

She knocked, expecting the door to open. She waited a moment, then knocked again, louder and longer this time. She heard footsteps and the same clicking sounds she had heard on the back door. She watched the door open and was greeted by an elderly gentleman with the longest white beard she had ever seen.

"Good morning. Mr. Fong is expecting you." The man motioned for her to enter. "Please, sit down and I will tell him you have arrived."

Lainey saw an oversized loveseat and couch covered in plush brocade fabric that looked as if it had never been sat upon. The two pieces faced each other with an elegant, dark wood, oblong coffee table between them. Each of the four legs had been carved to look as if a dragon, mouth wide open in a ferocious growl, were winding its way down to the floor. On the table sat a delicate tea service.

She sat down on the couch and instinctively ran her hand over the silky, soft material.

More extravagant and expensive decor. How is he paying for this?

She looked up to see a handsome man walking toward her. His black hair was pulled back in a ponytail. His waist length black sweater and tight fitting jeans gave the appearance he had just stepped out of an ad in GQ Magazine. She had to catch her breath when she looked into his eyes.

"Thank you for coming, Ms. Maynard," Ru said as he walked over to her. He put out his hand.

She stood up, put out her hand to accept his handshake. Instead, Ru took her hand into his and gently kissed the back of it. Her heart pounded.

Breathe slowly. In and out. Focus on the questions.

"Please, sit down. Make yourself comfortable." He positioned himself directly in front of her on the loveseat. "Would you like tea?"

Lainey sat down, trying not to stare directly at him.

"No, thank you," she said, clearing her throat.

He nodded and poured himself a cup of the steaming hot tea.

"I'm sure you are wondering why I asked you here."

"Yes."

Good grief, Lainey. Speak up. Is yes all you can say?

He smiled and took a sip of tea. Their eyes locked and Lainey couldn't avoid staring into his gorgeous green eyes any longer.

"Forgive me, but your eyes are the most beautiful shade of green," she began. "I noticed that Jillian has a similar eye coloring."

Ru put his cup back on the table, pausing as if he were contemplating his words carefully.

"I understand that you are investigating the unfortunate death of Brooks Helvig." He paused again. "I'm offering my assistance. I want to help you."

Lainey blinked several times before she spoke.

"How do you know that I'm inquiring into her death?"

"I have confidential sources, just as you do," he said with a grin.

"Why do you think I need help?"

"I respected Brooks. She did much to bring culture and the Arts to this small town. I wish to see that justice is done on her behalf."

She sat back on the couch, calculating her next words carefully.

"Have you spoken to the police?"

"I have a good relationship with our law enforcement officials. Have you spoken to them?"

She knew he was watching to see if she flinched. She worked hard not to.

"I will be talking with them soon. In the meantime, what is your connection to Jillian? I understand you met her in Mexico?"

"Our families have known each other for many years. She and I became acquainted with each other in Mexico."

"It's not common for two people from different families to have the same unusual green eye coloring, wouldn't you say?"

"Indeed. A rare occurrence I'm sure."

Lainey looked at her watch, knowing time was passing quickly. She needed answers.

"You are an experienced negotiator, Ru," she acknowledged. "If your offer to help is genuine, I need to know what information you have. My meeting with Jillian is at 10 a.m."

"Then you agree to my help?"

"I'm agreeing to listen to what you think might help me."

He nodded.

"It is my belief that Brooks' death was not an accident. I will walk with you to the Playhouse to meet Jillian. We can talk more confidently once you turn off the recording device you are wearing."

Crap! Who is this guy?

She felt her cheeks flush and she knew he could see the guilt written all over face.

"We should leave now in order to meet Jillian on time," he said.

He stood up, motioning with his hand for her to follow him.

She got up and walked to the door, waiting for him to open it.

"Is there something you need to turn off?" he said, holding on to the doorknob.

Reluctantly, she reached into her pocket and turned off the recorder.

He opened the door.

"After you," he said.

She walked past him, her pride a bit bruised, and angry with herself. He led her down the bright hallway, through the kitchen, and into the dining room. There were a dozen or more ladies in the room busily readying the place for the lunch crowd. None of them looked up or spoke as she and Ru walked to the front entrance.

"It is a nice surprise when visitors see the beads opening automatically," she said trying to end the awkward silence between them.

"We try to treat each guest with the utmost respect and that is one way to make them feel very special."

As soon as they left the restaurant and were walking on the sidewalk towards the Playhouse, Lainey stopped and turned to confront Ru face to face. She wanted to be on the offensive side now.

"I've complied with your request. Tell me what information you have."

"Many of your questions will be answered more fully when we speak with Jillian. I must ask that you trust me until then."

She looked at him for a very long moment before nodding in agreement.

She turned around, and they began walking toward the Playhouse once more. She saw a silver BMW parking in front of the building.

Wonder if that is Jillian?

"It is a beautiful day for a walk, don't you agree?" Ru said. "I enjoy a brisk..." His sentence was cut short by a loud, thundering sound. The sidewalk felt like a roller coaster speeding out of control. She was thrown backwards by a blast of hot wind that seemed to be as strong as a tornado.

When she woke up, her ears were ringing loudly, and her head was pounding. She wanted to stand but couldn't. What happened? Her vision was blurry, and she felt sick to her stomach. She thought someone was talking to her, but she couldn't hear or see them. Everything went black.

When she next awoke, she was in a hospital room, IV

poles beside her. People in scrubs surrounded her, all talking at once.

"What happened? What's going on?" She said as she tried to lift her head. It felt like it weighed ten tons.

"Try not to move. You are going to be all right. You have a concussion," someone answered.

She didn't have the strength to argue or ask more questions.

"Lainey?"

Mom? Is that you?

"Honey, it's Vera. Can you open your eyes?"

Slowly, she opened her eyes. Vera, Francy, and Della were standing beside her.

"My vision is blurry," she said. "And my head is pounding."

"Thank God you are alive!" Della said as she reached over to squeeze her hand.

Lainey kept blinking, trying to clear her vision. Her eyelids felt like heavy steel plates.

"I think my eyelashes hurt," she mumbled.

The ladies laughed.

"You're dang lucky you still have eyelashes, sweetie!" Vera exclaimed as a nurse came into the room.

"Hello, Lainey. Good to see your eyes open. I'm here to check your vitals."

"Why am I here? What time is it? I need to go to work."

"I'm afraid you won't be working today," the nurse said. She looked over to Francy. "Have you told her what happened?"

Francy shook her head from side to side.

"Well, our main concern right now is to get you feeling better."

"Let's give the nurse room to work," Della said as she

walked to the door. "She'll let us know when we can come back in."

The three ladies walked down the hallway to a small waiting room. Luckily, no people were inside. There was a coffee maker on the counter with a full pot sitting on the warmer and a Coke machine in the corner.

"I'm glad they have a pot of coffee on," Vera said. "None of the soda pop stuff for me. Makes me burp too much."

Della and Francy got cups of water and sat down at the one square table in the room. Vera joined them and the three were silent for a few minutes, each one trying to avoid what they knew needed to be discussed.

"She's up here with not one person to take care of her," Vera said as a tear rolled down her cheek.

"Francy, I think we need to tell her before your Captain Benson finds out she is awake," Della said somberly.

"Yeah, I agree. He's a great guy, but I've worked with him for a long time. He has very little bedside manner. He will question her and it's better if she's prepared for it."

Della nodded. She looked at Vera's trembling lip.

"I'm trying not to cry."

"Don't you worry, Vera. We'll take good care of her."

CHAPTER 8

Lainey's nurse walked into the waiting room. "You ladies can go back in now."

"Thank you. Do you know when the doctor is coming back by?" Francy asked.

"He usually makes his rounds early in the morning. We never know exactly when."

Francy nodded. She stood up, motioning for the two others to follow her. They walked back to Lainey's room and Francy stopped in front of her door.

"I'll tell her."

Vera and Della nodded, then followed her into the room to stand next to the bed. Lainey's eyes were closed until Francy gently touched her arm. Her eyes opened more quickly this time and she seemed more alert.

"Hey, are you seeing a little better?" Della asked.

"I think so." She looked at the three ladies. "They gave me something to ease my headache." Then she looked directly at Francy. "Tell me what happened. But first, can you raise the head of my bed just a bit?"

Della pushed the control to raise the head. "Tell me when."

"That's good. I want to see you as clearly as I can."

There was a pause as Francy looked first at Della, then at Vera, and then at Lainey. She took a deep breath in and let it out before she spoke.

"Do you remember anything from this morning?"

Lainey thought for a minute and said, "I fed Powie and I think I checked my email." She put her hand on her forehead. "Wait. Wait a minute. I had appointments, didn't I?"

Francy nodded. "Do you remember who with?"

"It was with Jillian."

Vera sighed. "Oh, honey."

"You were going to meet with her, but you had a meeting with someone else first," Francy said, trying to jog her memory.

"That's right! It was Ru. Ru Fong from the restaurant. I remember meeting with him, but..." Lainey blinked and rubbed her forehead. "I think he walked with me over to the Playhouse."

"Tell her," Della said forcefully.

"Jillian was killed this morning. Evidently she was parking in front of the Playhouse and when she turned off the engine, a bomb in her car exploded." Francy was watching her reaction very closely. "You and Ru were thrown backward by the blast from the explosion. You have a concussion from hitting your head on the sidewalk and may possibly have some hearing loss down the road."

Lainey opened her mouth to speak, but nothing came out. She closed her eyes and was silent. Her mind usually ran in overdrive feeding her ideas. But it was strangely quiet.

"Are you okay?" Vera asked. "We should have waited until you felt better to tell you."

"No, I wanted to know," she replied, opening her eyes again. "Was anyone else hurt? What about Ru Fong?"

Francy shifted her feet, shrugged her shoulders and said, "He was airlifted to Abbott Northwestern in Minneapolis and is in ICU. When he fell backward, his head and neck fell over the curb when he hit the sidewalk. He has a spinal injury and swelling in his brain."

Lainey shook her head slowly in disbelief. "I can't believe it."

"Neither can anyone else in Mirror Falls," Della said. "I think the entire town is in shock."

"It reminds me of the stories my folks told me about the gangsters in the '20s," Vera stated. "Not that I'm old enough to remember the '20s, mind you."

Francy rolled her eyes at Vera. "We know you're not that old."

"I think it's been a long day for all of us," Della began. "Why don't we let her get some rest. We can come back in the morning."

"You're right. I'm working tomorrow, but Mom and Della will be here until I get off."

"I'm so thankful you are here," Lainey said trying to grin. "I'll be better tomorrow."

The ladies each gave her a hug and started toward to the door.

"Francy?"

"Yes?"

"Your boss is going to talk with me, isn't he?"

"Yes, but don't worry about it tonight."

Lainey nodded. "Can you bring my computer here tomorrow? Or at least my cell phone?"

Francy grinned. "I'll check with the nurse."

The ladies left, closing the door behind them. The light had been dimmed and for the first time, she looked around the room. Other than the bed, a chair, and a tv mounted on the wall, it was empty. She wondered for a minute where her shoes were.

The door opened and the nurse peeked in. "Do you need anything?"

"No, I'm tired. Think I'll try to rest."

"We will be coming in every few hours to check on you. Press the call button if you need anything."

As the nurse closed the door, Lainey blinked several times, focusing on the hall light that shown underneath it.

Is the light moving? It's like fog being blown across a road or something.

She closed her eyes, hoping this was all a horrible nightmare that would be forgotten tomorrow. Della was first to arrive at the hospital the next morning and was surprised to see Lainey dressed and sitting in the recliner by the bed.

"Are they releasing you after just one night?"

"The doctor said they only wanted to observe me overnight and that I would get more rest at home than staying here another day."

"That's probably true," Della agreed. "How's the headache?"

"It's better, but still there. Now I know why my mom used to call me *the hard head* when she was mad."

They giggled as a nurse came in with the discharge papers.

"Here you are," the nurse said. "I still don't know how you managed to persuade the doctor to let you go home this soon."

Lainey shrugged and avoided looking at Della. "Just lucky, I guess."

"Yeah, lucky indeed," Della smirked.

The two walked in silence to the parking lot and were inside Della's car before Lainey dared to speak.

"Thank you for taking me home," she half-heartedly said.

There was no response.

"I know Powie will be happy to see me."

Still no response. Instead Della dialed a number into the car's Bluetooth and put it on speaker. A now familiar voice picked up. It was Francy.

"Hey, Della. How's our patient this morning?"

"She got herself released and is sitting here waiting for me to take her home."

"What? Are you kidding?"

"Hello, Francy," Lainey began in a very apologetic tone. "I'm really doing fine."

Della rolled her eyes and she guessed that Francy did, too.

"Do the police have any more information on poor Jillian?" She asked, hoping to change the subject.

"I need to put you on hold. I have a radio call coming in."

Lainey wiggled in her seat and tried to lighten the mood.

"Wouldn't it be fun if a song like *You've Got A Friend* played when you're put on hold?"

Della looked at her and after a long minute, smiled.

"Yes, I guess it might. I'm going to stay with you until at least afternoon, no arguments."

"No arguments. Thank you."

"I'll get in touch with Vera. She was heading to the hospital after her coffee time with Hazel."

Francy came back on the line.

"Lainey, Captain Benson wants you come by the office this morning for questioning. Do you feel up to it?"

"Can I get my notes from home and maybe change clothes first?"

"Be here by 9:30," she replied. "Della, I'll call Mom and let her know."

"Thanks, Francy. We'll run by her place and then head up

to the station. Is there anything else you can think of that she might need?"

"Not off hand. I've got to run. The switchboard has been going crazy this morning. See you later."

Della disconnected the Bluetooth, pulled out of the parking lot and headed for Lainey's apartment.

"It's almost 8:15," she said as she drove. "We need to hurry a bit. Good thing I don't mind violating the speed limit!"

"Aren't you worried about tickets?"

"No, I can usually talk my way out of them," she blinked several times, smiled, then laughed. "Of course, it doesn't hurt that Paul knows everyone."

Speeding was an understatement. The trip from the hospital to her house would normally take five or six minutes. Della made it in under two minutes.

"Whoa," Lainey said, sliding from one side of her seat to the other each time Della turned a corner. "And I thought I drove fast!"

"Paul says we need to develop a new game app," she laughed. "He wants to call it Della's Curvy Swervy Auto Derby. Catchy, don't you think?"

Lainey smiled and then frowned.

"My car is still parked behind the Chinese Palace and my garage door opener is inside."

"Paul and I drove it home yesterday for you. I have the opener on my sun visor. We fed Powie, too."

"That was very kind of you. Thanks."

"Not a problem. You haven't known us long, but you are a part of our group now. We help each other."

Della opened the garage door and the two got out of the car. Lainey opened the utility room door and paused.

"My alarm was on yesterday. How did you figure out the code to shut it off?"

"You forget where Francy works. We opened the door

which set off the alarm. Then we waited for the alarm company to contact the police department. Francy intercepted the call, told them it was a false alarm, and to turn it off."

"Remind me to stay on her good side," Lainey grinned. "I might need backup someday!"

Within a half hour, the two were back in Della's car, heading to the police station.

"Your eyes still look bloodshot. Is your head hurting?"

"It's a dull throbbing, but not too bad. I am having a hard time tuning out the ringing in my left ear. Sometimes it's loud, sometimes not. It should get better in a few days."

Della pulled into a parking space fairly close to the front of the station. Lainey was surprised by the size and appearance of the building. It had three stories and resembled a courthouse that would have entertained dignitaries during colonial times. The wide concrete steps led up to the second-floor main entrance. There were two large pillars holding up a massive roof that covered the area from the stairs to the doors.

"This looks like a state capitol building," Lainey remarked as they walked up the stairs toward the door.

"It was built in the '20s, I think. In fact, a couple of men from either Dillinger's or Capone's gang were arrested and spent a few days in the jail on the third floor. There's talk about designating the building as a historical site and building a new station."

That ties in with the photo I saw online showing two of Capone's men being arrested at Miss A's Saloon.

They opened the heavy door and were met by two officers manning the entry.

"Good morning. Please, put your purse, keys, belts, or anything metal in the plastic bowl on the counter," the officer directed. "Then proceed through the detector."

They did as he instructed, gathering their items on the other side of the device. The second officer motioned for them to come forward. He was holding a clipboard.

"What is the reason for your visit today?" the officer asked politely.

"We have an appointment with Captain Benson," Della replied.

"Please sign your name and the time of your arrival. I'll let him know you are here."

The officer used the radio clipped to his vest to let the captain know his visitors had arrived.

"Captain Benson will be here shortly to escort you to his office. There are benches on either side of the hall if you'd like to sit down."

"Something is going on," Della whispered to Lainey as they sat down. "I've never had to walk through the metal detector. In fact, I can't remember seeing officers at the door before either."

"Security must have been tightened after the incident yesterday."

"Makes me a bit uncomfortable."

The two sat quietly watching the officers watch them. Footsteps soon echoed in the hall as Captain Benson approached.

"It's good to see you up and around, Lainey," he said shaking her hand. "I see you brought reinforcements."

Della smiled. "Good to see you. Paul said you bowled a 289 last week."

"If only I hadn't opened in the tenth." He gave her a hug.

"Let's talk in my office." They walked down the long corridor and climbed the stairs to the third floor.

"My office is the first door on your left. The jail takes up the rest of this floor."

"Where is Francy's station?" Lainey asked as he unlocked his office door.

"She's down the hall in the jail control room. Please come in and make yourself comfortable. Della, I have to ask you to wait outside."

"I'll see if Francy is busy. Let me know when you're ready to go."

"She'll let you know," the captain said as he closed his door.

Lainey sat in one of the two wooden chairs in front of the captain's desk. The seat was as hard as a rock. The officer sat down at his desk, turned on a small black desk lamp, and leaned back in his chair.

"Thank you for coming to speak with me. I realize you've been through quite an ordeal."

Lainey nodded. "I was planning to meet with you yesterday after I met with Jillian..." her voice trailed off.

"This is not an interrogation and you are certainly not a suspect. The seriousness of the events in Mirror Falls over the past few weeks cannot be ignored. I am aware that Herman Helvig hired your company to investigate the murder of Brooks and the life insurance policy that was to be inherited by Jillian. Is that correct?"

"Yes, sir."

The captain paused briefly. "It's been said that I come across as harsh at times. That is not my intent. So, don't take offense when I say that I don't have the luxury of beating around the bush. Tell me all that you have so far in your investigation."

For the next few minutes, Lainey explained about her meeting with Helvig at the Playhouse and his apparent hatred of Jillian. She didn't mention the hidden room she had seen or what she had learned about Miss A, the brothel, or the redacted report Helvig gave her.

"And I was to meet Jillian yesterday to get her side of the story."

The captain, who had leaned forward while she was talking, sat back in his chair mulling over the information.

"And you met with Ru? Did you get a chance to question with him?"

"No. I met him briefly in the restaurant. He suggested we walk over to the Playhouse to meet Jillian."

The captain nodded slightly. Then he opened the top right-hand drawer of his desk, took something out and placed it on the desk. He stared at Lainey.

That's my pocket recorder! I forgot all about that!

She reached to pick it up, but he stopped her.

"We found this on the sidewalk where you fell."

"I was carrying it when I met with Ru. He realized I had it and made me turn it off."

"So, you haven't listened to what's on it?"

"No. But evidently you have."

The captain picked up the device and said, "I'm amazed it wasn't damaged. We did listen to it and you are right, he did ask you to turn it off. There wasn't anything of use on that portion of the recording."

Lainey looked puzzled. "What do you mean? What else is on there?"

"Two partial sentences that we can make out." He turned the volume up and hit play.

The tape was scratchy and the sound of sirens in the distance muffled the words even more.

"Unfortunate… not target. Family ties."

Lainey eyes opened wide.

"Family ties? Is that what I heard?"

"We think so. Why?"

"The other day I found a fortune cookie taped to the

steering wheel of my car. The paper inside it had the words *family ties run deep*."

The silence between them was interrupted by the ringing of the phone on the captain's desk.

"Yes," he answered forcefully, listening intently.

"Bring up what you have, immediately," he ordered and hung up the receiver. "I've been in law enforcement for almost thirty years, seven of them as a captain. I've been in Mirror Falls my entire career," he paused. "My grandfather was chief of police when Miss A opened the brothel."

CHAPTER 9

Lainey looked surprised. "What? Helvig said..."

"That my grandfather was a customer of Miss A? That he was a crooked official?"

She nodded. "He alluded to that."

There was a knock on the door and a man dressed in plain clothes stepped inside the room.

"Here is the latest report, sir." The man nodded to Lainey and handed the folder to the captain.

"This is Detective Wang. He has been working on this case for a long time. Detective, this is Lainey Maynard."

"Nice to meet you," the detective said, holding out his hand. "I'm glad you weren't seriously injured."

"Thank you," she replied, shaking his hand.

"Wang, Ms. Maynard may have information to help with your investigation. Grab a chair."

The detective sat down in the other wooden chair as instructed. He looked at Lainey, then at the captain.

"I apologize, but I'm somewhat confused here," she began, sitting forward in her chair. "You've been investigating Helvig? Why? I was told he was an upstanding citizen."

"We have reason to believe that Helvig is involved with a very powerful drug smuggling cartel that might also have ties to a human trafficking operation," the detective said.

Lainey had been trained to keep a poker face and not show her hand in situations like this. But this time, she couldn't. She was shocked and immediately felt the blood rush into her face and her left ear began ringing loudly.

"In Mirror Falls?" she asked.

The detective nodded. "We've known Mirror Falls is a main corridor for running drugs from Mexico to the Twin Cities area for a long time. From there, it's disbursed to dealers nationwide."

Lainey shook her head in disbelief. "Living in Houston, I knew Texas had a major drug smuggling problem, but I never dreamed drugs would be smuggled through the Midwest via Minnesota."

"We have been working with the DEA. They've been watching this cartel for some time. They feel it's a powerful organization with advanced technological capabilities."

"In Mexico?"

The captain cleared his throat. "The connection may originate from China."

China? Miss A?

Lainey's mind was racing. She sat forward in her chair, waved her right hand and said, "Wait. Let me try to understand this. The drugs being smuggled are coming from China?"

The captain smiled. "Detective, want to field that question?"

"Sure."

Wang described an operation so complex even Einstein would have had a hard time understanding it. He began by saying that China is a main source of what is known as precursor chemicals that are used to manufacture drugs such as heroin, cocaine, and crystal meth. In fact, China is a major source of ephedrine and pseudoephedrine.

The plant that is used to produce these chemicals, known as ephedra, grows wild in some parts of China. They are also a leading exporter of bulk ephedrine to many countries, including Mexico. Once the bulk shipment hits a Mexican port, it is directed through an elaborate maze of warehouses, finally landing in hidden manufacturing plants or sites. It's then made into the drug of choice and the process of smuggling into the US begins.

Lainey stared at the detective, trying to take in all the new information.

"How does human trafficking tie in?"

"Brothels have been used to cover up female human trafficking for a long time," the captain stated. "Ai Jiao Ju, or Miss A, did exactly that. Her family was one of the most powerful and ruthless drug cartels in China at that time. We believe she was sent to Mirror Falls to manage that part of the family business in the US."

The three were silent, each one waiting for the other to speak. Finally, Lainey broke the silence.

"Is it possible that Miss A's family also had activities in the drug smuggling between China and Mexico?"

"Absolutely," Detective Wang said. "We feel it was a turnkey operation. Export the precursor chemicals to Mexico, control the manufacturing side, then arrange for the drugs to be smuggled into the US. The prostitution of young girls provided a perfect way to blackmail their families in China, corrupt government officials in Mexico, and wealthy businessmen."

"And law enforcement in Mirror Falls," Captain Benson added.

The intense ringing in Lainey's left ear had lessened and she was beginning to feel more like herself.

"I see how the Playhouse ties in, but not how Helvig fits into the picture."

"We haven't found enough evidence yet, but we feel he is a main player in the money laundering side of this operation," Wang stated.

"We need to work together on this," Lainey said. "I know I can help you."

"I agree. But you will have to follow my rules. I call the shots, understand?" The captain commanded. "This investigation is bigger than any one person or department. Helvig will lead us to the head of the operation, I'm sure of that. We have to be very careful. He is an intelligent man."

"Agreed," she said, nodding to the detective and the captain. "We've talked about everyone except Ru Fong. What is his involvement?"

"That's what we were hoping you would find out. We don't have much information on him at present."

Lainey thought for a moment. "I do have a small amount of information on him at home that my company's Tech Supervisor found on him. Do you want me to bring it by?"

"Yes. Detective Wang's office is on the second floor. How soon can you bring it?"

"Tomorrow morning? I'll talk with my office and see if there is any additional information."

"I'm in the office by 8 a.m.," the detective said. "I'll let the officers know you will be coming early."

The captain stood up, signaling the meeting was over. He walked around the desk and extended his hand to Lainey. She stood up and shook his hand.

"Thank you for coming. I think we will be working together for a long time."

"I hope so, captain."

"Wang will walk you back downstairs. I'll let Della know you are ready."

He opened the door, nodded at the detective, and then went back to his desk.

"We can wait for your friend in the hall," Wang said. "Follow me, please."

Lainey left the office and felt suddenly very tired. She yawned as they waited for Della.

"It's normal to feel tired after a traumatic brain injury or concussion. Drinking water and resting will help tremendously," the detective advised. "My son had a concussion last year."

"From playing football?"

"No, his older sister was practicing kick boxing and he was the punching bag."

Lainey grinned. "I'm sure it was an accident."

The detective laughed. "She's at least a foot shorter than him and weighs about one hundred pounds. I doubt drop-kicking your brother for making fun of your new boyfriend's picture is considered an accident."

Della and Francy came out of the jail control room door and greeted them.

"Hello, detective," Francy greeted. "This is Della Kristiansen."

"Ah, another Whoopee member, correct?" He said, shaking her hand.

"Whoop, whoop!" Della replied, laughing. "Guess we are the local celebrities!"

Francy rolled her eyes. "Or just around the station anyway."

"I need to get back to work. I'll take your friends downstairs, Francy. Ladies, please follow me."

"Call you later this evening, Lainey," Francy said.

The two friends didn't talk as they followed the detective downstairs. They walked past a line of people waiting to go through the security station and the two officers they had seen earlier. Neither said a word until they were in Della's car, where they both spoke at the same time.

"Did Francy say…"

"What did the captain…"

The two chuckled. "You go first," Lainey said to Della, who had started the engine. "I'll have to hold on for dear life until you get to my apartment."

They laughed loudly. "At least you're honest about it. Paul just closes his eyes and prays!"

The trip back to Lainey's house took no longer than the trip to the station.

"See, I *did* get you home safely," Della remarked, sitting down at the small kitchen table. "Got any coffee?"

Lainey smiled. "I'll make you a cup. What did Francy have to say?"

"Not much. Between the jailers coming and going from the control room, she couldn't talk freely. But she did say the town's gossip mongers were busy spreading rumors."

"Rumors about Jillian?"

"And Helvig and Brooks," Della paused. "And you."

Lainey smirked. "I figured. What's being said?"

"Now, remember, most people don't yet know who you are. Don't take any of these rumors seriously. It's just busybodies butting in where they shouldn't."

Hmm… obviously not a complimentary rumor to say the least.

"What in the world are they saying?"

"That perhaps you were seeing Ru Fong."

"They meant I'm having an affair with him?"

Della nodded. "It's just a rumor. Most of the town's people don't believe that bunk."

"Here's your coffee," she said, placing the hot cup down on the table. "I put dark chocolate syrup in it for you."

"Nice! Have a seat and tell me what the captain had to say."

Lainey sat down across from her and tried to summarize what was said. She hadn't been able to write notes but mentioned the drug smuggling and possible human trafficking of young girls.

"I'm going to take the information I have to Detective Wang in the morning and ask for a copy of the information they have."

She was interrupted by the ringing of the internet phone in her office.

"Crap! I haven't checked in or told Snoops what's happened!"

"Who is Snoops? A spy or something?"

"He's the most experienced researcher in the home office. I swear he can find anything. I'm sorry, Della, but I need to call him back. Can we talk later?"

"You bet. I'll bring your cup back next time I see you."

"Thanks."

"Go make your call." Della gave her a hug, took her cup, and left through the utility room door.

Lainey was turning on her computer when she heard a knock at the front door. She looked through the window to see Della standing there holding a box.

"Just a sec," she yelled to Della. She unlocked the door and the glass screen door.

"I forgot to give you this. It came FedEx yesterday while Paul and I were here. He signed for it."

She handed a small, square box to her.

"Thank you."

I'll bet it's the new cell phone. Glad I have it before I call him back.

Lainey closed the door, opened the box and saw the iPhone inside. When her computer was ready, she dialed the internet phone and waited for Snoops to answer.

"Sorry I missed your call. Have you found more information for me?"

"Who is Paul Kristiansen?"

"Oh, he and his wife were visiting me yesterday. I got busy cooking and he signed for the phone you sent me."

He's not going to buy that. It even sounds lame to me.

"Call me back when you're ready to be truthful." The phone line went silent.

"Geez, he hung up on me," she said while dialing him back. The phone rang several times before he picked up.

"Don't get angry, I didn't think you knew," she said quickly.

"I always know. How are you feeling?"

"I'm tired, but better. Who told you?"

"Your phone should be ready to go. You may need to charge it."

That's just great. He's not going to tell me. I need to watch what I say and to whom I say it.

"I'm emailing information on Helvig and money laundering. Call me back when you've read through it. I'm sure you will have questions. In the meantime, I have more information on Miss A."

Lainey found a notepad and pen. "I'm ready. What have you found?"

"Ai Jiao Ju's family did send her to the US to run their drug and human trafficking operations. Her family grew much of the opium smuggled out of China and controlled the exporting of it at the time. They kept the brothel supplied with young girls by threatening the men who worked on their farms with death or dismemberment of all their family members if they didn't surrender their daughters on demand."

Snoops paused, typing on his computer, then continued. "Are you following so far?"

"Yep."

"Miss A either built a new connection in Mexico or strengthened an existing relationship, I'm not sure. It appears her daughter, Li Jang, was sent to Mexico to be raised and groomed to eventually control the operation there."

"Who's the birth father of Li Jang?"

"Nothing on him. Whoever buried his name doesn't want it to be found."

"Do you have names of the partners in Mexico? When did Li come back to Minnesota?"

"We found more than a dozen different company names, addresses, and fake postal records. Li Jang did give birth to Annchi Bao in Minneapolis in 1955. Again, there is no evidence of the birth father's name. Tracing the records we have uncovered of Miss A's travels, it appears she and Li Jang travelled to Minnesota together from Mexico, perhaps for the child's birth."

"So, Annchi Bao is Miss A's granddaughter. The blood line continues with females, did you notice that?"

"Not sure that is relevant, but yes, it crossed my mind."

"What do you know of Annchi?"

"We are checking into what looks like a physical examination report when Annchi was born. If we are correct, Li Jang died shortly after she gave birth. If that is true, Miss A most likely raised her granddaughter. I'll keep looking for more information on Annchi. We have confirmed that Miss A died in 1980."

Lainey was silent, trying to jot down notes.

"Thank you, Snoops. This investigation into a simple life insurance fraud claim has certainly taken a turn, hasn't it?"

"I warned you that this was dangerous and to not take things lightly. Jillian's murder is evidence of that."

"Sadly, I realize that. Have you found anything on her background?"

"A few things that I have not verified yet. I will let you know when I have it. When are you planning on speaking with Captain Benson again?"

"In the morning. He wants me to bring the information you've uncovered. Maybe it will shed light on his investigation."

"Print the Helvig information out, read it tonight, then take it tomorrow for your appointment."

"I'm to drop off the information with a detective that has been working on the case."

"Do not give this information to anyone but Benson."

"I'll call him first thing in the morning and ask for an appointment."

"Show up at his office at 9:30 a.m. He'll be there to take the information."

"Okay," she answered hesitantly. "You're sure he will be there?"

"Still questioning my instructions?"

"No, no, sir. I'll be there."

"Good. Check in with me tomorrow. Hopefully I will have more for you."

"You got it. Thanks again."

"And, Lainey, we're all glad you are okay. Be careful."

"I will."

She hung up the phone. Powie had been walking around her chair, purring and meowing.

"Hungry? Let's get you some food." She walked into the kitchen and filled his bowl. She opened the fridge to find something to eat and saw a mason jar full of chicken noodle soup. A sticky note on the front read *My homemade chicken noodle soup will perk you right up. Love, Vera.*

Lainey smiled.

I'm sure it will, Vera. I'm sure it will.

She hungrily finished the soup, cleaned up the kitchen

and returned to her computer. Clicking on the email with the Helvig information, she opened the attached file, started reading, then stopped. Feeling completely exhausted, she decided to print the few pages and shut down her computer for the night.

"C'mon, Powie. Let's hit the sack," she said as she walked into the bedroom. "I think I could sleep for a week."

CHAPTER 10

The loud ringing of her cell phone woke her the next morning. She rolled over, grabbed the phone and said in a sleepy voice, "Hello?"

"You still sleeping?" Francy asked.

Lainey yawned, still trying to wake up. "What time is it?"

"It's about seven in the morning. I thought you would be up by now."

"It's seven? I can't remember the last time I slept that late."

"You've had a rough couple of days. I can call back later if you want to go back to sleep."

"No. I'm awake. Are you working today?"

"I'm off. Can we talk before you head over to the station?"

Lainey's mind cleared, and for a second, she panicked, thinking that she was going to be late. Then she remembered Snoops changed the time of her original meeting.

"I'm to be at the station by nine-thirty. Can you come here around eight? I need to shower and get dressed."

"You bet. Maybe I can help with the case. See you in about an hour."

"Sounds good. See you soon."

Lainey quickly got ready, took care of the cat duties, and had the Keurig on when Francy knocked on the front door.

"Come in, it's open."

Francy walked in, took off her shoes, and gave Lainey a hug. "Sorry if I woke you."

"No problem. I needed to get up. How about coffee?"

"Sure. Did you like Mom's chicken soup?"

"It hit the spot. Please, thank her for me when you see her."

The two sat down at the table, sipping their coffee. Lainey watched Francy's face and could see she was debating whether to say something.

"What is it, Francy? You can tell me."

"I can't verify this, but you've stumbled into something that's more than just a murder case. And the scope of this may go far beyond Mirror Falls."

Lainey nodded. "Captain Benson told me as much."

"No one, other than the captain and Detective Wang, had any idea that Herman Helvig was being investigated or that the DEA was involved."

"Is it unusual for an investigation to be kept secret from the rest of the department?"

Francy paused to think about the question. She took a breath and blew it out, making a whistling sound.

"Well, that depends. While the main details of an investigation may not be known by many, it is common knowledge about what investigations are ongoing and who in the department is handling them."

"Della mentioned that she hadn't seen officers screening people coming into the station before. Is it not done on a regular basis?"

"The last time security was in place at that entrance was when the Governor came here for the fishing opener in 1984."

"Fishing must be a big deal up here," Lainey chuckled.

"You have no idea!"

"Why security measures now? Because of the Helvig investigation?"

"The car bombing has caused more damage than an earthquake measuring 9.9 on the Richter scale. This sleepy little town's residents were oblivious to the corruption outside the city limits. After all, crime only happens in big cities, right? Suddenly, every John Doe is hearing on the local news about two murders of prominent people, and an explosion that left a well-known restauranteur fighting for his life and injured a woman investigator sent here from Texas."

Lainey sighed. "Yeah, I see what you mean."

"You'd think John Dillinger's gang was back in town. People are frightened."

"Can't the captain do a press conference or put a statement out to ease their minds?"

Francy shrugged her shoulders. "Benson was here when I started working at the department. He was a patrol officer then and didn't socialize much with the others. In fact, for several years, the only time he talked to me was to radio in his status or if he needed something. Don't get me wrong. He's a good cop and follows procedures to the letter."

"Maybe he's trying to prove something," Lainey mumbled, thinking out loud.

"Prove what? His record is stellar."

"Did you know that his grandfather was chief of police?"

"I think I heard that. Back in the '30s. Why?"

"Brooksey's Playhouse was a brothel back then run by a Chinese woman known as Miss A. I understand she entertained law enforcement officials in exchange for protection for her operation."

"Oh, man. You think his grandfather was one of her customers?"

Lainey put up her hands and shrugged. "It's possible."

"Talk about a black spot on a family's reputation. Guess we all have skeletons in our closets we want to hide."

"True. Give me your honest opinion. Do you think I can trust him? He wants all the information my company has found."

Francy paused for a long while, tapping the top of her coffee cup. She took another deep breath and said, "Two days ago, I would have said absolutely. Why are you hesitant?"

Lainey got up, walked into her office and picked up a folder lying on her desk. She took out the papers, made copies of them, and walked back to the kitchen.

"I haven't read this yet, but if the captain isn't on the up-and-up, I need someone else to have my back. I'm not wanting to jeopardize your job, and I understand if you don't want to get involved. But I trust you."

The two sat in silence, looking at each other. Francy sat back in the chair, rubbing her chin. Then, leaned forward and slapped her hand on the table.

"I've had a good feeling in my gut about you since the first time we met. Mom calls it my intuition antenna. My brother used to call it gas."

The both laughed and smiled.

"So, that means you'll help me?"

"I'm in. Tell me what you have so far."

Lainey shared with her the information about Miss A, her family's history of smuggling drugs and trafficking young girls. Francy stared in shock when she heard their operations spanned several continents and countries.

"Captain told you all that?"

"Actually, Detective Wang did most of the talking. The captain listened quietly."

"What about these papers?" Francy said, holding up the copies.

"I haven't read them yet." She looked at her watch. "I need to scan them quickly before I head over to the station. My meeting is at nine-thirty."

They were silent as each read their copy. Francy kept shaking her head as she read.

"Unbelievable. Here, in Mirror Falls."

Lainey nodded.

"Tell you what," Francy stated, putting down her copies. "I'll go up to the station while you are meeting with him. I'll figure out a way to search for more information."

"How? You're off today. Won't they think it's odd for you to just show up?"

"I've got some of Mom's sugar cookies in my freezer. They're used to her bringing treats for the break room. I'll say she wanted me to drop them by."

"She's a real gem, isn't she?"

"There's never a dull moment when she's around. Now, I'd better go so you won't be late."

"Let's go out the garage door," Lainey said. She picked up the file and put it in her backpack along with her iPad.

"Glad you have the alarm," Francy said as she walked out the door.

"Me, too. Be careful, my friend."

Lainey got in her car and watched Francy drive away. She adjusted her rearview mirror and said to her reflection, "You've got this." She backed out and headed to the station.

The parking lot was much emptier than yesterday, and she was able to park close to the entrance. The security check area was manned by the same two officers, asking her the same questions in the same monotone voice.

Talk about major déjà vu. It's like I'm in the Twilight Zone or something.

She sat down on the bench, waiting once again for Captain Benson. Instead, Detective Wang walked up.

"Do you have the information for me?"

Lainey thought quickly.

"Actually, I'm supposed to meet with Captain Benson instead."

The detective straightened his shoulders. His voice became a little less friendly.

"Who authorized that meeting?"

Okay, Lainey. Now what do you say?

"My home office."

The detective stared at her. She knew he was trying to intimidate her or make her feel uncomfortable. She held his gaze, glad she was wearing her backpack with the file safely inside.

"Wait here."

He turned and walked away. Lainey glanced over at the two officers who had been listening to her short conversation. Their stony faces didn't give her a warm, fuzzy feeling either.

The bench she was sitting on resembled a church pew. She scooted as far back in the seat as she could, securely squeezing the backpack between the bench and her back. She crossed her arms and waited.

Minutes passed. Lainey didn't move, keeping her gaze squarely on the end of the hallway. Detective Wang finally reappeared, but instead of walking to meet her, he simply gestured for her to follow him. She stood up, making sure she had a hand on the front strap of her backpack, and walked toward him. Before long, she was once again sitting on the rock-hard chair in front of the captain's desk. But this time, he wasn't in the room. Wang stood silently by the open office door as if he were guarding it. She turned toward the door when she heard footsteps in the hall.

"Sorry to keep you waiting," the captain said as he came into the room. "It's been busy this morning." He sat down behind his desk, looked at the detective and nodded. Detective Wang left the office, closing the door behind him.

Lainey watched while the captain shuffled through a few papers on his desk. He stood up, walked over to the other wooden chair, and turned it to directly face her chair.

Show you're not weak here. I can play musical chairs, too.

She stood up, turned her chair slightly, and sat back down. The two faced each other, their chairs about two feet apart.

"You have spunk," he said curtly. "And some influential pull, I might add."

"I'll take that as a compliment."

"Don't. This investigation is escalating rapidly, and you happened to be in the wrong place at the wrong time. Show me the file."

Lainey eyed him for a moment. Carefully taking off her backpack, she opened it, took out the file, and handed the papers to him.

"I want my recorder back."

"It's evidence."

She studied his eyes as he read through the file but couldn't tell if he was surprised by the information or was already aware of it.

"This ties in perfectly with what we've found about Helvig being involved in the money laundering side. How familiar are you with Bitcoin?"

"I believe it is digital currency that was created by someone using an alias of Nakamoto or something similar."

"It's called cryptocurrency and is used to conduct money transactions without banks or other traditional institutions being involved. You can make purchases anonymously from anywhere in the world. International payments can't be connected to any country, and so far, it's not regulated."

"Don't people buy it as an investment, hoping it goes up in value?"

"Some who believe the dollar bill will go the way of the old silver certificates might see it as an investment. However, the Dark web's large criminal markets have taken advantage of the anonymity it provides them and their customers. You can buy everything from fake passports, drugs, guns, and hacked credit cards to assassinations."

Lainey blinked. "Criminals purchase assassinations with Bitcoin?"

"Of course. No regulations, no bank transaction trails, and it is completely anonymous. Many of the criminal websites closely resemble the ones found every day on Amazon or eBay. These sites are very user friendly and we've found that they even ask for customer reviews."

"Wow. So, Helvig used Bitcoin to launder money?"

The captain seemed to relax a little bit. He smiled.

"Money laundering is an extremely intricate and technically involved process. Depending on how large an operation is, there could be hundreds of people involved in one laundering scheme."

They were interrupted by a loud voice in the hallway.

"I've got sugar cookies!"

The captain leaned forward in his chair.

"I don't suppose you *knew* Francy was dropping cookies by?"

She shook her head. "Not a clue."

He nodded toward the door. "I think you could use a break."

He stood up, walked to the door and opened it.

"After you."

Lainey smiled and walked into the hallway.

Look out Francy. I don't think he's buying it.

CHAPTER 11

She followed the captain down the hall to the jail control room door. He punched in a code on the electronic pad beside the door and waited for the loud clicking sound that signaled it was unlocked. He held the door open and she went inside.

The room wasn't large. The walls were painted battleship grey and the air smelled of burned coffee and tuna casserole. A counter in the shape of a square filled the middle of the room and left only a narrow walkway around it. Three desks inside the square faced a wall of windows overlooking the prisoner's recreation room. A row of television monitors was perched above the windows, each screen videoing a different prison cell.

"Welcome to the tank," Francy said as Lainey walked in. "I didn't realize you were here."

"Coincidence, huh," Captain Benson stated flatly, crossing his arms as he leaned against the counter.

"This is Officer Hudson, the jailer on shift, and Sandy Carell, dispatcher," he said casually. "Guys, meet Lainey

Maynard, insurance investigator and new resident to Mirror Falls."

"Hello, it's nice to meet you," Lainey said. "I appreciate the service you do for us."

"Nice to officially meet you," the jailer said. "Although we did meet a couple of days ago."

"We did?"

"I was off and heard the call about the explosion on my home radio. I helped load you into the ambulance."

"Oh, thank you. I'm sorry I don't remember much about that."

There was brief, awkward silence. Lainey looked at Francy as if to say, "Do something."

"Mom insisted I bring these cookies up to the jail. She knows sugar cookies are a favorite,"

Francy grinned. "Want one, Lainey?"

"Sure." Francy handed her the Tupperware container holding the cookies and Lainey grabbed one.

"Captain?"

He shook his head no. "I'll get one later. Right now, if *you* have no objection, we have a meeting to conclude."

"Yes, sir. I'll make sure to save you a couple," Francy replied.

The captain and Lainey left the control room and walked silently back to his office. They sat down in the two wooden chairs, still facing each other.

"Let's cut to the chase," he began. "Your research and ours confirm that a couple of forms of money laundering are happening. The first form is known as smurfing. Some of the drug money or dirty money went from China to Mexico and then was split up into small sums of cash and deposited into many different accounts to avoid detection. Some of the dirty money was cleaned by using various currency exchanges, wire transfer, or cash smugglers called mules.

These mules smuggle very large amounts of cash across the borders of foreign countries that have less strict or undetectable money laundering safeguards."

"And you think Helvig was the brains behind all this?"

"Not exactly. We think Helvig's involvement revolves around commodities such as gold or gems. He set up shell companies that could easily move these commodities into other forms of investments. These corporations, which only exist on paper, invest in and sell assets such as real estate, counterfeiting, and gambling organizations."

Lainey leaned forward. "What about jade? Could he have used jade?"

"Yes, many gemstones could be involved. Why do you ask about jade?"

"I saw a large jade globe on his desk when I met with him. Jillian had a jade Buddha sitting beside her computer screen, too."

The captain was silent, and she could see he was considering this new information.

"Why haven't you arrested Helvig?"

"Arresting Helvig will not put a stop to the main cartel's operations. He's actually a small piece of the total operation. We've been trying to get him to lead us to the top of the organization. Now that two murders have occurred, the DEA has elevated this to a high priority."

"What can I do to help?"

"Stay away from Helvig. Lay low and don't bring any additional attention to yourself."

Not the words Lainey liked to hear. She bit her bottom lip to keep from responding.

"The only time I want to see you is if you have additional information from Mr. Clyde Bedlow," he said, almost daring her to say something.

Her eyes narrowed. She took a breath, then slowly replied, "If you don't hear it from him first."

"Glad we understand each other. I think you can find you way back downstairs. I'm sure Francy is there waiting for you."

She nodded, got up and turned toward the door. Before she opened it, she looked back at him and said, "What did you say your grandfather's name was?"

He didn't respond.

She smiled. "You have a great day, sir." She walked out the door, down the stairs, and saw Francy sitting on the now familiar bench.

"Let's go outside," Lainey said quickly. The two walked past the security and out to the parking lot.

"I don't feel comfortable talking here. Meet me at Caribou Coffee," she said. Francy nodded. They got in their cars and headed for the shop. Lainey watched to see if Francy was following her. She was not. She parked in Caribou's lot and went inside. To her surprise, Francy was already sitting at a table.

"How'd you beat me here?"

"I know all the short cuts," Francy smiled. "He knew why I was there, didn't he?"

"I'm pretty sure he did."

"I thought so. That's why I left. Sorry, I didn't get a chance to find out any information."

"It's okay," Lainey said, looking around at the people in the shop. "I'm hesitant to talk in public and to be honest, I'm a bit hesitant to talk at my house."

"We could go to Mom's. I'm sure it's safe there."

"Will she mind?"

"Nope. She loves having company."

The two left the shop and got in their cars. Lainey

followed Francy to Vera's house, her mind filled with questions. How did Helvig get involved with this Chinese cartel in the first place? Why did he despise Jillian and why did they both have jade on their desk? Why kill Brooksey? And what is the connection with Ru? Was he Jillian's boyfriend?

She pulled into Vera's driveway behind Francy. They got out and were greeted at the door.

"Come in, come in," Vera said, hugging them. "I've got coffee brewing and just put a tater tot hot dish in the oven to heat."

Lainey grinned. "Tater tot hot dish?"

"It's a Midwest thing," Francy chuckled. "It's a hamburger casserole topped with tater tots."

"I see. It sounds good."

"Take your shoes off and come on into the kitchen," Vera said. "Excuse my mess, but I've been addressing church welcome cards all morning and haven't had a chance to straighten up."

The three sat down at the small table, drinking coffee and waiting for the casserole to heat up.

"I was hoping the sugar cookies would disguise my reason for being at the office," Francy said, but the captain saw right through it, didn't he?"

"You didn't take those old frozen cookies? For Pete's sake, they probably tasted like cardboard. I'll make a new batch for you."

"Mom, that's not necessary. The cookies were fine."

"I have a reputation to maintain you know," Vera said proudly. "I'll make a batch and take them up myself."

Francy looked at Lainey and rolled her eyes.

"What did he say to you?"

"I'm sure he knew you were there to help me out. I'm sorry, but I don't trust him."

"Captain Benson? Why he was the nicest young man on the force. Doc knew his family," Vera remarked.

"Dad knew everyone in town," Francy replied. "People change, Mom."

Vera shrugged. "I guess so, but his mother would turn over in her grave if she thought he was treating people badly."

Lainey was glancing out the kitchen window, looking at the wind blowing the tree branches, when she suddenly turned to Francy with a surprised look on her face.

"Holy cow," she said. "It's like a light bulb just turned on in my brain. He's not embarrassed by his grandfather's affair with Miss A. I think he's hiding something else that could destroy his career."

It was Francy's turn to look surprised. "What? You think he's a part of all this?"

"I'm beginning to." She told the two ladies about the suspicion of money laundering and Helvig's alleged involvement.

"Captain Benson said that gold and gems were investments that could easily be used by shell companies to buy and sell assets like real estate."

"You mean Helvig created companies that took gems purchased or obtained with dirty money and paid for investments with the gems?" Francy questioned.

"I'm not an expert, but I think that is what Benson was saying. I'm going to talk with my company resource person and make sure."

"How does that make you think the captain can't be trusted?"

"Helvig had a round globe, resembling a large paperweight, sitting on his desk. He told me it was jade. The night we left Brooksey's Playhouse, I stopped to talk with Jillian, remember? I noticed sitting by her computer desk was a jade

Buddha." Lainey leaned closer to the table. "And have you ever noticed the ring on the captain's right hand?"

"Holy Cow! It's jade!" Francy exclaimed.

Lainey nodded in agreement. "Exactly. It sure looked like jade."

Vera had been oddly quiet, listening intently to the conversation. Her cheeks lost their rosy color and she stood up slowly.

"Mom? Are you all right?" Francy asked.

Vera nodded yes and walked out of the kitchen. Francy and Lainey looked at each other.

"Should you go after her? I didn't mean to upset her."

"Mom?" Francy called out.

"Just a minute," Vera yelled. "I'll be right back."

From the kitchen, they could hear closet doors and dresser drawers being opened and closed hastily. Finally, Vera appeared carrying what looked like a music box. She sat down at the table, placing the box in front of her.

That box has the same red dragons on it as the waitresses' kimonos at the restaurant!

"What's that?" Francy asked. "I've never seen it."

"There's a lot of things you haven't seen, dear," Vera said. "I had forgotten about this." She rubbed her hand over the smooth top of the shiny box. "When your father started his medical practice, many people were farmers who couldn't afford to carry medical insurance. Your father, bless his heart, never refused to treat anyone, regardless if they were able to pay him or not."

She opened the box and gently removed the contents, cradling it in her hands.

"Bertha Benson, Lee's mother, had been a widow for some time."

"Lee is the captain's first name," Francy added.

Vera continued. "Lee and his older brother were swinging

from a rope that was tied to the roof of the barn, trying to see who could swing the highest. The brother either lost his grip or the rope snapped. He fell two stories to the ground, breaking his arm."

She paused. "He suffered a brain injury and was never quite the same. Your dad went to the farm every day for weeks to check on him. Bertha was so grateful, she gave him this box. She said it was all she had."

Lainey stared as Vera laid a golden brooch delicately shaped like a flower on the table. Each petal was intricately detailed and at the center of the piece was a large, shiny green gem.

"It's jade," Vera said. "Bertha told him it was an old family heirloom. I've never had the heart to wear it."

Francy's mouth dropped wide open. She looked at Lainey and then back at the brooch, still a bit speechless.

"Who knows you have this?" Lainey questioned, suddenly worried about Vera's safety.

"No one, I guess. Doc never talked about his patients and Bertha's been gone a long time."

"May I take a picture of it with my phone? I want to send it to the home office."

"Sure. Think I should give it to the captain?"

"No!" Francy and Lainey said loudly in unison.

Startled, Vera's lip began to tremble. "Well, golly, you don't have to scream at me."

"Mom, we didn't mean to yell at you. Until we know if there is a connection between this brooch, Helvig, and the captain, the best thing you can do is put it back where you had it and forget that it's there."

"I agree, Vera. Now is not the time to be mentioning this to anyone."

"Okay, if you think that's best," Vera answered. She put

the brooch back in the box and left the room to put it back in its hiding place.

"Did you notice the dragons on that box were the same as the ones we saw at the restaurant?" Francy whispered.

"Yes, and I don't think it's a coincidence, do you?"

"No, and I can't believe the captain is involved."

"We don't know that for sure. He said the investigation was moving very rapidly and if we are going to find out anything, we'd better work on it now."

Vera walked back into the kitchen and said, "Work on what?"

Francy and Lainey exchanged glances, neither knowing how to respond.

"Girls, I may be old, but I'm not deaf. I've been around the block a time or two. What's the plan?"

Over the next hour, the ladies tried to figure out the best way to gather information on the jade connection. They talked about asking Della to do some research on the computer for bloodlines or information on Bertha's relatives.

"Snoops, the guru in my company's home office, has resources checking into the Dark web and he is having trouble finding any information. I'm sure Della would find nothing."

"Why is his internet dark? Mine is slow, but it's never been a dark color," Vera asked innocently.

"The Dark web is a name for hidden criminal networks and activities. Very few people can access it," Lainey explained trying not smile.

"That's exactly why I only use that darn computer to play solitaire and cribbage. I swear I feel like it knows the moves I'm going to make before I make them!"

"I have a valid reason to talk with Helvig again," Lainey began. "I'll tell him it's to wrap up the investigation he hired us to conduct. I want to at least take a picture of the jade on his desk and see if the Buddha is still by Jillian's computer."

"You can't ask for a police escort or backup either," Francy added.

"What if I go along?" Vera asked.

"Out of the question, Mom. How could you help?"

"She might need a get-away driver. I could park down the street just in case."

Lainey thought it over and said to Francy, "That might not be a bad idea."

"If we were both in the car, I could text you if something was happening outside," Francy suggested. "Mom in the car would give me a good excuse if someone questioned what we were doing."

Vera crossed her arms. "Told you I could help."

Not the greatest idea, but I think it's all we've got right now.

"Okay," Lainey agreed hesitantly. "Is there anyone in the department you trust that we could ask to be on standby?"

Francy thought for several minutes. "A girlfriend of mine is married to a Sheriff's Deputy in Stearns County. They are here for the week moving her mother into a senior living apartment. If we needed him, he could get to us in a few minutes."

"Think it's safe to tell him what we're doing?"

"No, I'm not going to alert him ahead of time. But I'm sure if I call his cell with an emergency involving Mom, he'll respond in a heartbeat."

"I'm a very good actress. After all, I was the female lead in my high school performance of *Wuthering Heights,* you know," Vera added. "I can fake a heart attack easily."

They would have laughed at her response, but the seriousness of what might happen weighed heavily on each of them. Lainey took her cell phone from her pocket and looked at her friends.

"I'll call Helvig and see if he can meet as soon as possible. Be quiet so he doesn't suspect I'm with anyone."

Francy's palms were sweating and Vera was rocking back and forth silently in her chair. Lainey put the phone on speaker and dialed the number. It rang several times before Helvig picked up.

"I was waiting for your call. Obviously your services are no longer required."

"Hello, Mr. Helvig. I do need to meet with you as soon as possible. It won't take long, but I am required to do an exit interview confirming we have completed the job you hired us to do."

There was no immediate response.

"I'm sure you want to wrap this up as quickly as possible," she added.

"I'm at the Playhouse. Be here in twenty minutes. Call when you get to the front entrance."

"Thank you, sir. I'll be there."

She hung up the phone and looked at the two ladies. "How soon can you be ready?"

"The Playhouse is eight or nine minutes' drive from here. You park in front and we will park far enough behind you that Helvig won't see us when he opens the door."

"Okay. Have your friend's number ready if you have to call him." Lainey walked toward the front door with Vera and Francy following.

"Lainey," Vera said, stopping her before she left the house. "Be careful. We have your back."

"Don't take any chances with Helvig, get the heck out of there if you sense any danger," Francy said.

"I will. If all goes well, when you see me walk back outside to my car, wait a minute or two to follow. I'll meet you back here."

Her heart was pounding as she got in her car. Taking

several breaths to try and slow it down, she noticed her backpack still in the front passenger seat.

If the Buddha is still there, maybe I can sneak it into my backpack without Helvig noticing.

She started the car, backed out the driveway, and headed to the Playhouse. When she was close enough to see the building, she noticed the barricades guarding the area damaged by the explosion. She drove past the entrance, made a U-turn and parked on the opposite side of the street, still directly in front of the entrance. She felt sick to her stomach as she got out of her car and walked past the broken pavement where Jillian's car had been. The burn stains and residue were still visible on the curb and the front of the building. She pulled out her cell phone and dialed Helvig's number.

"I'm here," she said when he answered.

He said nothing but hung up the phone. Lainey didn't dare look to see if Francy's car was parked down the street for fear that Helvig might see her and be suspicious. She stood in front of the big entrance door, backpack in hand, trying to look as confident and comfortable as possible.

Helvig walked to the door and opened it only far enough for her to squeeze through, then closed and locked it.

"Thank you for seeing me on short notice."

He didn't answer and instead, began walking toward the office where she had first met him.

"Let's go to my office."

Lainey nodded, looking over at the counter where she had spoken with Jillian.

I need to get over there.

"My apologizes, but my phone is vibrating. I'll turn it off and be right there," she said, hoping he wouldn't stop and wait for her.

"Hurry up, I'm busy," he said continuing to walk ahead. "You know where the office is."

She quickly walked over to the ticket area, praying the Buddha was still there. She looked over the counter, picked up the statue and hastily threw it in the front zipper pocket of her backpack.

She hurried down the foyer to Helvig's office. He was sitting at the desk, typing on his computer when she walked in.

"What do I need to sign to get rid of you?" he said without looking up.

"If you could write a statement saying you are ending the investigation and are satisfied with our service, I would appreciate it."

"I'll email it to you."

Thinking quickly, Lainey replied, "I do have specific questions for you to address in the statement. I've found that clients feel it more convenient and less time consuming to type responses as we talk."

Helvig stopped what he was doing and looked at her with an expression of great annoyance plastered all over his face.

"Lucky you weren't standing closer to the blast," he said with a smirk.

"And lucky you weren't opening the door for Jillian that morning."

His eyes grew narrow and his expression turned stony.

"I've dealt with know-it-all, conceited dames ten times tougher than you. Let's just say their gift of gab has been silenced."

The tension in the room was stifling. Lainey walked closer to his desk, trying to show confidence and trying to locate the jade globe on his desk.

"The first question: Did our agency provide you with accurate, timely information?"

She stood as tall as her 5'4" frame would allow.

He studied her for a long time before he spoke.

"I'll answer your question when you sit down."

She nodded and moved the padded chair to the left of his desk till it was sitting was directly in front of the desk. Then she sat down.

CHAPTER 12

"How long has she been inside?" Vera asked Francy nervously.

"I'm not sure. We hit every darn stop light coming here and she was already inside when we parked."

"I don't like this. Not one bit. Is it time to call your sheriff friend?"

Francy was watching the street in front of her car, the building entrance, everything and anything that might be moving. Her cell phone was in her right hand. She looked at it and hesitated.

"Not yet. Let's give her a couple more minutes."

Vera sat back in the passenger seat, glancing at her side view mirror. She jerked forward, put her left hand on the seat and rapped on it hurriedly.

"There's a car parking behind us," she said, continuing to stare into the mirror.

Francy looked first into her side mirror and then moved her eyes over to look in the rearview mirror.

"Don't panic, Mom. Just sit still. We don't know who it is."

The black car behind them had tinted windows making it

impossible to see who was inside. Francy hit the lock button on her door making sure they were as safe as possible.

"Come on, come on. Where are you?"

Meanwhile, Lainey sat staring at Helvig, determined to wait him out.

I can sit here as long as I have to.

Helvig finally broke the link between their gazes and returned his attention to his computer screen. He began typing. She saw the jade globe sitting beside a picture of Brooksey and tried to think of a way to get a closer look at it.

"What else do I need to write?" he said angrily.

"If you were satisfied with the results you received and if would you recommend our services."

He typed quickly, then stopped. The printer in the far corner of the room beeped three times.

"It's printing," he said. He stood up and walked to the printer. Lainey saw an opportunity, stood up and grabbed the jade globe, intending to put in it her backpack.

She felt a hand squeeze hard on the back of her neck.

"Check her hands, Hermie," a man's voice stated.

Helvig turned around, his grin as big as a Cheshire cat. "Caught with your hand in the cookie jar?"

The man, still holding onto the back her neck, forced her to sit down while Helvig walked back to his desk.

"You're the most ignorant excuse for an investigator I've ever seen," he scoffed as he sat down. "She's not going anywhere." He motioned for the man to let go of his grip.

Lainey rubbed the back of her neck and watched as Maxie Payton walked over and stood beside Helvig.

"Apparently, you value my jade globe more than you value your life. So, be my guest. Take a good look," he said, smiling up at Maxie. "You're not going to own it for much longer."

Lainey looked down at the globe in her hand, praying

silently that Francy had called for help. She took a breath and said with as much disgust in her voice as she could muster.

"You sent him to break into my apartment."

"Maxie had no intention of coming inside that night. The object was to scare you into installing an alarm. Let's say he installed free upgrades to your system."

"The zones in your apartment have undetectable listening devices. Every time you opened your mouth, we heard you," Maxie said smugly. "You lead a boring life."

Keep them talking... need to buy time till help arrives.

"How did you know Miss A?"

"*Know* her? She's the reason I'm wealthy today. Your friend, Snoops, didn't fill you in?"

Lainey blinked her eyes.

"If you were listening, you know he didn't."

"He's not as bright as he thinks he is either. My people followed him all through the Dark web, blocking him at every turn. I'm a very powerful enemy and I have hundreds of loyal workers that will do whatever I ask."

Lainey wiggled in her chair.

"Maxie," Helvig said, keeping his eyes on Lainey. "Did you detain her friends as I asked you to?"

"They're sleeping very soundly," he replied, winking at Helvig. They both laughed.

Oh dear God, let them be all right... please let them be all right.

"You've been trying to play hard ball with the big boys. It's comical really. We had you on a string since I called your company. I let you dance when I desired it. Now," he yawned, "I'm tired of you. Take her downstairs."

Maxie tied her hands in front of her, put some sort of tape over her mouth and pushed her out the door. She knew the room Helvig was talking about. It was the secret room underneath the Playhouse. Her mind was racing, panicking, and trying to figure some way out.

Maxie opened the black door, pushing her in front of him. Her legs felt so heavy she could hardly move them. Slowly they descended the cold winding staircase until she stood facing the steel door she knew led to the hidden drug den.

He grabbed her arm and opened the door as if it were as light as a feather. He shoved her inside.

"Helvig must like you. He let me kill the other women he had down here. I guess he wants you to stay alive a little longer." He laughed loudly and walked out the door, closing it behind him.

Lainey's eyes couldn't adjust to the deep darkness of the small room. She instinctively walked toward the wall where she thought the light switch might be located. The stench of the room was burning her eyes and nose. She cringed as she put her face against the wall, running it up and down, hoping to feel the switch and raise it up with her chin.

Suddenly, she stood still.

Keys! Someone's putting a key in the door!

For a moment, panic overtook her. What if it was Helvig? What if Maxie had changed his mind and had come back to kill her?

Her body stiffened as she stared toward the sound of the lock being turned. Slowly, the heavy door opened. She saw a small figure step inside, then close the door behind them. She could hear the person walking closer to her and stop. The light suddenly flashed on.

Lainey blinked repeatedly, trying to let her eyes adjust once more. She felt a touch on her shoulder and a voice whispered, "You are safe, child."

She blinked once more and saw an older woman standing in front of her, gently removing the tape from her mouth. Tears filled Lainey eyes and she tried to speak, but she choked on the putrid odor in the room and began coughing.

The woman patiently waited for her to catch her breath and reaching inside her pocket, pulled out an object that resembled a letter opener.

"We will talk in a moment," she said as she quickly cut through the binding holding her wrists.

Lainey lunged forward, hugging the woman. "Thank you, thank you, thank you," she said tearfully.

The door opened again. "We must go," a man urged.

The woman nodded and taking Lainey's hand, led her through the doorway. She stopped in front of the stairs, waiting for the man to close the door once more. Lainey stepped forward, eager to get upstairs to safety, but the woman stopped her.

The man moved away from the door, knelt down and touched a stone very close to the base of the stairs. The woman stepped up onto the first stair, motioning for Lainey to do the same.

The man, still kneeling, knocked on the rock floor. Immediately, a portion of the floor began to raise up.

"A trap door?" Lainey said out loud.

The woman smiled. "A door to life."

When the door had raised completely, she saw stairs leading down to a brightly lit hallway.

The man helped the older woman down first, then Lainey. He followed, making sure the door above them was closed.

"Our family has used this tunnel for many years. It serves our purposes well."

Lainey, still trying to get a grip on everything that had happened, nodded.

"Who are you?"

The man behind her said, "She is the granddaughter of Ai Jiao Ju."

I know that voice!

She stopped and turned around.

"Yes, I am the man who greeted you when you came to see Ru," he said, bowing slightly.

"Now, we must continue on. We are almost to our destination."

They walked in silence for several more minutes. Lainey was trying hard to piece things together. When they finally came to the end of the tunnel, the man stepped ahead of her and the woman to open the door. There were no stairs behind this door. Instead, there stood an elegantly designed multi-paneled screen painted with flowers, birds, and trees. The man quietly slid the screen to one side revealing an elevator behind it.

They entered and quickly rode upwards. When the door opened, Lainey was stunned to find she was standing in Ru's elaborate office.

"Oh my Lord!" She blurted out. "Francy and Vera! Do you know if they're safe?"

The woman nodded. "They are being attended to and will be fine."

The emotions from the evening finally overtook Lainey. She put her head in her hands and cried.

The woman patted her on the shoulder and led her to the brocade couch where she had sat during her meeting with Ru.

"Jin, would you please bring tea?" The woman asked. She sat down beside Lainey. "Tears will cleanse not only your eyes, but your heart."

Jin returned quickly with the tea. He placed the tray on the coffee table in front of the couch, poured a cup, and handed it to the woman.

"It will calm you," she said, sipping her tea.

Jin poured a second cup, handed it to Lainey, and sat down across from them.

Lainey's hands were shaking as she lifted her the cup to her lips. The tea felt warm going down her throat. She looked at the woman.

"Is your name Annchi Bao?"

The woman smiled. "It is a pleasure to meet you. Finish your tea. Jin will provide answers for you."

She took another few sips and put her cup back on the table.

"Thank you for saving me," she began. "How did you know where I was?"

"That is not important at present. What is important is that you know Annchi's family has not been involved in the drug trade for many, many years," Jin said. "Should I continue?" He asked Annchi.

"Jin's family has served as guardians for my family for generations. He is kind and faithful." She smiled at him. "His family has sacrificed their own lives to protect us. My ancestors were rich and powerful and did indeed deal in the trade of opium," she paused. "And the selling or trading of young Chinese girls. I am not proud of that history, but it needs to be said."

Lainey nodded. "Miss A, your grandmother, did she operate the brothel as a front for your family's drug trade?"

"Yes, she did until 1949 when her son was killed in a raid in Mexico."

"She had a son?"

"Liu Jia was two years younger than my mother, Li Jang. Ai Jiao was ordered by her father to have her children raised in Mexico by Jin's ancestors. She grieved her son's loss for a long time and became very bitter. She was the only living family member connected to the illegal smuggling operations and when my mother died only days after I was born, she cut all ties to the business in order to protect me."

Annchi finished her cup of tea and placed it back on the table.

"Would you like more?" Jin asked her.

She shook her head no. They were silent for a moment. Lainey noticed how graceful Annchi was and how devoted Jin was to her.

There was a soft knock on the door before it opened.

"Hello, Mother," a man said as he walked in. Lainey stared in disbelief as Detective Wang walked over to Annchi and kissed her on the cheek.

"Forgive me for being rude when we last met," he said to Lainey as he walked over to sit down beside Jin. "Hello, Father."

Lainey knew they could see her shock and confusion by the expression on her face. But she couldn't help it. She sat there, stunned.

"My given name is Lang Chao. I have been watching Helvig from inside the police department as Detective Wang. Francy and Vera are safe. We followed their car and intercepted Helvig's man before he could hurt them."

"Maxie Payton?" She asked.

"Helvig has many hired men. Payton is the one closet to him."

"My dear, you have been through much this day. It was not my desire for you to be involved," Annchi said. "Herman Helvig is an evil enemy."

Questions were crowding every inch of Lainey's mind as she listened and tried to regroup her thoughts.

"How did he become involved with your family?"

Jin and Lang Chao looked at each other, then at Annchi. She held up one hand, nodded and smiled.

"My grandmother raised me in the traditions of our culture. She told me of my family's dark history when I became old enough to understand," Annchi paused. "She worked very hard to distance herself from the family's illegal activities. However, there was one man who had known her as Miss A and had worked for her in a small part of the operation. When my grandmother chose to cut her connections, this man became angry. He not only took control of the organization, he retaliated against my grandmother by murdering my mother."

"I'm so sorry, Annchi, I had no idea."

"It was a very long time ago. While many of my family in China have passed away, I still own the mining operation."

"Jade. You mine nephrite or jadeite to make jade," Lainey said as she made the connection.

"Yes."

"I still don't know how Helvig fits into the picture."

"The man who had my mother killed was Herman's grandfather."

Lainey's jaw dropped. "Helvig's been laundering his family's drug money using the jade made from your mines!"

"It's more involved than that, but yes, that's basically it," Lang Chao said.

"There is one more thing you need to know," Annchi said, looking at Jin as if to get his approval. "My grandmother and I, along with Jin and his family, came back to Mirror Falls in order to stop their operation. Herman's father and grandfather had died, and he had never seen my grandmother or me."

"Annchi went to work at the same bank as Helvig in order to watch him closely. Even though he was married, he was a womanizer and raped several of the girls employed by the bank," Jin said angrily.

Lainey's eyes grew wide. "He raped you?"

Annchi nodded. "He gave me a gift, a daughter."

Silence enveloped the room. Jin stood, walked over to Annchi and put his hand on her shoulder.

"Herman found out about her, and in order to protect my child, my grandmother gave her to one of Jin's sisters to raise as her own. When my child was only a month old, a man broke into his sister's home and beat her. He injected a lethal dose of heroin into her arm when he left."

It's Jillian!

"Jillian was your daughter?" Lainey asked, a bit dumbfounded.

Annchi smiled. "She was a beautiful child."

"Ai Jiao thought Jillian would be safer if she were raised by someone with no connection to our families. It was arranged for the Blumpkists to adopt her," Jin said softly. "We quietly moved back to Mexico, keeping communications open with Joe and Marian. Our plan was to return when Jillian turned eighteen."

"My mother sent money to them for Jillian's education," Lang Chao added. "When they were killed, Ru brought Jillian to us in Mexico."

A small tear glistened in Annchi's eyes. "Ru is also our son. He and Jillian inherited my grandmother's green eyes."

Jin patted her shoulder and said, "His recovery will take a long time, but he is being treated by the best physicians."

Lang Chao's cell phone rang. He saw the number, stood up, and walked into the other room to take the call.

"When did you start the China Palace?" Lainey asked.

"Helvig became more powerful and greedier. He began using more and more of our resources in his illegal laundering operation. We moved back to Mirror Falls and opened the restaurant. Herman had no idea Annchi and I were living here, nor did he know about Ru or Jillian," Jin explained. "In order to go undercover, if you will, Lang Chao joined the police department, Ru managed the restaurant, and Jillian developed a relationship with Brooks."

"Our intricate plan to expose Helvig was working," Lang

Chao said as he came back into the room. "Until Brooks tried to help my sister by purchasing a life insurance policy and naming her the beneficiary."

"She was a good-hearted person," Annchi stated. "I think she truly wanted to provide for Jillian."

"When did Helvig learn Jillian was his daughter?"

"He became suspicious as soon as he met my sister. He hired a private investigator to find out about her. Brooks had no idea that her husband was involved in illegal activities and we think she talked with him in detail about Jillian. She considered her the daughter she never had."

"It was her green eyes," Annchi said softly. "My grandmother had green eyes."

"Did he kill his wife over a million dollars? I'm sure he pockets ten times that much or more."

"The life insurance policy was not the reason he killed his wife," Lang Chao stated. "He realized Jillian's connection to him and to our family and if she was the heir to the mines supplying him jade, he had to get rid of her."

"We think he was trying to frame my daughter with Brooks' death," Annchi said. "He began putting very tiny amounts of cocaine in his wife's coffee, which I understand she drank three or four times each day."

"Jillian regularly met with Brooks at her home for coffee and to talk. He planned on using those visits as evidence that my sister was drugging her in order to take sole possession of the Playhouse. That would provide ample suspicion to have her arrested on murder charges. He had no knowledge of the insurance policy until after she died," Lang Chao commented.

"That's when he called my company to investigate," Lainey said.

"He thought you were going to provide him with an ironclad way to make Jillian appear guilty of murder," Annchi finished.

"Were you aware he was recording your first meeting with him?" Jin asked.

"No," she hesitated before continuing. "I'm embarrassed to admit that I wasn't thinking as clearly as I normally do when I interview clients. He took me to the underground room before he would talk with me. I was caught off guard, shocked and angered. I never thought he might be recording our conversation."

Lang Chao nodded. "That is exactly what Helvig did with every woman he felt might be a threat to him. He used that room to intimidate you which gave him the advantage."

"He said that room played a part in his wife's death. Is that true?"

"I believe it is time to go to the restaurant," Annchi said, standing up. "Come with us. We will talk more."

CHAPTER 13

Lainey watched as Jin took Annchi's hand and walked beside her to the door.

He cares so much for her. I think he would do anything she asked.

"I'll follow behind you, Lainey," Lang Chao said.

They walked into the hallway, made a few turns and entered the restaurant through the kitchen back door. The room was busy with men and women cooking, washing dishes, folding napkins, and chopping vegetables. They worked with such precision. Groups of people were coming and going, like a school of swiftly swimming fish. It was amazing to watch.

Jin led them through a set of double doors into an area filled with closets and small vanity tables with lighted mirrors attached.

"This is where our hostesses dress for work," Jin said. "Each one has her own space to keep personal things."

They continued through the dressing room and into a small room not as lavishly decorated as the main dining area Lainey had seen before.

Jin pulled out a chair for Annchi and she sat down. He motioned for Lainey to sit next to her.

"This is where we share our family meals," Annchi said, waiting for Jin to sit on her other side.

"Lang Chao, would you please ask a few of the girls to join us?" He nodded, leaving the room.

"How did you like our food when you ate with us?" Annchi asked.

"It was delicious. The atmosphere of the room was very hospitable, and I was so impressed with the waitresses."

"Annchi trains each one," Jin said proudly. "She has the grace of a swan."

Her son returned quickly with three young girls. They had been the ones folding napkins in the kitchen. They bowed slightly when they entered and smiled.

"May I introduce Cara, Sarah, and Elaine," Annchi said.

"Very nice to meet you,"Lainey greeted, a bit surprised that their names weren't Chinese.

The girls nodded. "You and your friends sat at my table a few days ago," Elaine said.

"Cara and Sarah are sisters. Their mother was abducted and sold as a prostitute to a wealthy Asian client of Helvig's. She died shortly afterwards. He held the sisters hostage in the same underground room where we found you," Jin said.

She looked at the beautiful young girls, shaking her head in disbelief.

"A man broke into my house one night," Elaine began. "And my screams woke my mom. She bravely fought the man who was trying to molest me. I saw him hit her over and over again until she fell to the ground. She never moved. He threatened me to remain silent about what happened, or he would kill me."

Annchi watched Lainey as she covered her mouth in horror.

"We know the man was Max Payton," Lang Chao said bitterly.

"I'm so sorry," Lainey said to the girls. "That is awful."

The girls looked at each other and smiled.

"Miss A saved us. We're very happy here as part of her family," Elaine said.

"Thank you, girls, that's all we need for now," Jin said, dismissing them.

Lainey stared at Annchi. "*Miss A*? They call you Miss A?"

"Indeed," Lang Chao said. "My mother has rescued hundreds of young girls and women that have felt the effects of Helvig's thugs. She brings them here, nurses them back to health, provides schooling, and loves each one of them. They become our family."

Annchi sat quietly in her chair, watching the girls leave. "You see," she said gently. "The tunnel *is* a door to life."

Lainey could only stare in amazement at this proud, humble woman. "Did you rescue all of the girls here?"

She nodded. "My grandmother taught me well."

"May I ask if you know why Helvig killed Jillian?"

"Max Payton killed my sister. He had been stalking her for weeks. He was hiding in the theater the night you talked with her after the play. She was the last one to leave the building. He followed her to her car and tried to assault her. Luckily, she carried mace with her. She kicked him and then sprayed the mace in his eyes. That allowed her to get in the car and drive off," Lang Chao stated.

"We think he planted the bomb on her car sometime later that night," Jin said.

"You mean to get even with Jillian?" Lainey asked.

"Evil thrives on retaliation. She had bested him, and he was determined to get even," Jin stated sadly.

"I was there when Helvig arrived on the scene. He was clearly angry that Jillian's death ruined his plan to blame her for Brooks's murder," Lang Chao said. "He didn't care that she was dead or that she was his daughter."

Annchi sighed. "It is getting late. The restaurant will open soon."

"If you know all this, and you can prove Helvig's guilty, why don't the police arrest him?"

There was a pause before Lang Chao answered.

"Helvig can lead the police to his main financial supplier, who is much more powerful. My mother and father wish to remain as anonymous as possible. Coming forward or accusing Helvig now would only bring attention to them and jeopardize the future of the girls they have worked hard to help."

"I understand," Lainey said as she stood up to leave. She turned once more to face Annchi.

"I am forever grateful that you saved my life. If there is any way I can ever repay you..."

Annchi shook her head. "Come by the restaurant often. I will know when you are here."

She hugged Lainey and walked out the door.

"If you come to the police station, remember, I'm Detective Wang," Lang Chao smiled.

"You got it."

She left the restaurant and to her surprise, her car was parked in front of it.

How did they manage to move my car?

She got inside and took a deep breath. "I'm ready to go home," she said out loud. She started the car and drove quietly. As she pulled into her driveway, Max Payton's words, *every time you opened your mouth, we heard you,* hit her like a brick wall.

"I can't stay in that apartment," she said thinking out loud. She backed out and headed for Vera's, hoping Vera was home. She parked in the driveway, looking for a light that might indicate someone was inside. She got out of her car, locked the doors, and walked up to the front door. She rang the doorbell, then knocked. Vera opened the door and seeing Lainey, threw up her hands and yelled, "Francy, she's here! She's here! We have been so worried about you!"

Lainey walked inside and they hugged each other. "What in the world happened to you? Where have you been?" Francy asked.

"I'll tell you, but first I'm so glad you two are okay. I thought you might have been hurt."

"We're fine. Detective Wang was on patrol and saw us parked. He told us a sting operation was going down and the road was going to be closed. I had to tell him we were waiting for you. He said not to worry, he'd let you know."

Thank you Lang Chao!

"Can I stay at your house tonight, Vera?"

"Of course you can! We'll have a sleep over. I've got popcorn and coffee. We can play cards if you like, but at 10 p.m. I watch the *Golden Girls*."

Lainey smiled. "Thank you. I really appreciate it."

For the next hour, Francy and Vera sat at the kitchen table listening to the unbelievable turn of events that Lainey was describing.

"He bugged your entire apartment?" Francy stated. "That gives me the creeps."

"I'll call a different alarm company from the cities tomorrow. I'm through with ADT for a while. Do you work tomorrow?"

"Yes, I'm on days."

"Would you call… oh poop! My cell phone is in my backpack and the last time I had that was in Helvig's office."

"Don't worry, you can buy one of those cheap phones at Walmart tomorrow. And forget about retrieving anything from Helvig's office."

"I agree with you. He'll find out I'm not a prisoner and I need to be prepared when he does."

Francy eyed her for a long minute. "Ride with me to work in the morning. You'll be safe at the station. And you can catch the captain before the shift change briefing."

Lainey nodded. "Can we stop at my apartment and feed Powie on the way?"

"Of course. Is he okay this evening?"

"He should be. I filled his food and water before I left this morning." She yawned. "Man, that seems like years ago instead of hours ago."

"Honey, you must be exhausted. The spare bedroom is the second door on the right and the bathroom is directly across from it. Go, get some rest. I'll wake you for breakfast," Vera said. "I'll make pumpkin pancakes and eggs!"

"Thank you. I won't forget this."

"Piddle! That's what friends do," Vera smiled.

Lainey hugged Vera, then Francy, and headed down the hall to the spare bedroom. The bed had a fluffy, maroon comforter that looked so inviting, she laid down and immediately fell asleep, still wearing her clothes.

The next morning, she awoke up to the sound of Vera singing *You are my sunshine, my only sunshine,* and the smell of coffee and pancakes. She smoothed the wrinkles out of the comforter, ran her fingers thru her hair, and walked into the kitchen. Francy was sitting at the table, getting ready to pour maple syrup on a stack of cakes.

"Morning," Lainey said. "Smells so good." She sat down and put two pancakes on the plate in front of her.

"Mom's the best pancake chef in town but watch out for her homemade chokecherry syrup. It's got a bite!"

Vera smiled broadly. "It's certainly popular at church. Last Sunday, I brought a whole jarful to put on the muffins during the coffee hour. There wasn't a spoonful left."

"I'm not rushing you," Francy said. "But we need to get going."

Lainey nodded, quickly eating the last couple of bites on her plate.

"You girls go ahead, I'll clean up the dishes," Vera said.

"Thanks, Mom. I'll call you later."

They hurriedly walked toward the front door to put on their shoes. Francy opened the door and turned to Lainey.

"I'll drive. You'd better leave your car here, just in case."

"You're right. Helvig and Payton know my car, that's for sure."

Francy drove to her apartment, stopping long enough for Lainey to feed her cat, and then headed to the police station.

"I'm usually here by 6:15 a.m. My shift starts at 7, but I like to get caught up on what happened during the last shift. The captain usually comes in about the same time."

Once again, the entrance had two officers manning the security station. Francy waved them off. "She's with me. I'm checking in for my shift." Lainey followed closely behind her as they walked upstairs to the jail control room.

Francy punched in her code, held the door open and motioned for Lainey to go ahead.

"We need to talk," a voice barked before she could take a step inside. Captain Benson was standing with his arms crossed, blocking the doorway. "Turn around and go to my office. I'll be there shortly."

Lainey glanced toward Francy. Her face looked like someone had thrown a glass of cold water in it. She turned to walk back to his office as he said, "The sergeant will handle this morning's briefing. Don't call me unless someone's dead."

"Yes, sir," Francy said as she walked inside. "Will do."

The captain's footsteps were loud and deliberate, and he

caught up with Lainey in a flash. He opened the door and said, "You know the drill. There's the chair."

How does he know? What does he know? I hate this hard chair!

"You were told to stay away from the Playhouse and from Herman Helvig," the captain said angrily. "What don't you understand? I told you he was dangerous."

"I know, but... "

"I'm not finished!" He yelled at her. "You could have ruined our entire investigation, besides the fact that you could have been killed. Do you know how many people have been working on this? You waltz in here, think you know more than I do, and I'm the one having to clean up your mess!"

Lainey sat in silence. The captain glared at her, then got up from his chair and walked over to his desk. He picked up her pocket recorder that he had kept as evidence and, looking directly at her, clicked the off button. He set the recorder back on the desk, walked back over to the chair, and sat down. He smiled at the confused look on her face.

"I... what... I... " she stammered, staring at him.

"I had to be convincing. I do have a reputation, you know," he grinned. "I am upset with you, but I'm also very glad you're safe. You got a lot more than you bargained for yesterday, didn't you?"

She nodded. "How did you find out?"

"My mom was a wonderful woman and she loved my dad a great deal," he paused. "His family was very close and a month after he died, a card arrived addressed to Mom." He carefully took the jade ring off his finger. "My dad's family wanted mom to know she would always be a part of them and cared for." He handed the ring to Lainey. "Do you see the connection?"

She held the ring, looking at the beautiful jade oval in the middle. "Are you related to Miss A?"

"Ai Jiao Ju loved my grandfather and he loved her. But because he was the chief of police, he couldn't publicly make that known. Instead, he vowed to always protect her. She gave him this ring. It was passed down to my father and then to me."

Lainey smiled. "The jade meant that he was a part of her family, didn't it?"

"Yes. And the card sent to my mom had only four words: *family ties run deep.*"

Her mouth opened. "You know about Annchi, the restaurant, and Jin?"

He nodded. "We are very close. And like my grandfather, I can't allow that relationship to become public. You understand that if you ever mention this, I will adamantly deny it and," he looked over at the recorder on his desk and smiled. "I have proof of how much dislike I have for you."

She handed the ring back to him. "I hate you, too," she said, grinning.

"Good," he chuckled. "Now, back to Helvig. We know that your visit alerted him that his cover had been blown. And I'm waiting for the official go ahead to issue a warrant for him and Max Payton."

"I'm sorry if I caused problems with the investigation. I was trying to piece together his relationship with Jillian."

"Go back to Vera's until your home alarm system has been replaced. You are much safer there."

"You know about the alarm being bugged?"

"I'll have Francy take you back to her mom's house. Stay there. Bake cookies with Vera or play cards. But you must stay there. I think you know the seriousness of the consequences if you don't."

"I'll stay. I do need to stop and get a phone. My home office is probably wondering why I haven't checked in."

"Snoops is aware of what has occurred. He agrees that you need to stay put. The phone can wait."

"Is there anything you don't have access to or control of?" She asked.

"I haven't been able to control the weather… yet." He said with a sly grin.

CHAPTER 14

The rest of the day was uneventful. Lainey and Vera drank coffee, played Uno and dominoes, baked German chocolate brownies for the station, and drank more coffee.

"It's been nice spending the day with you, Vera."

"Consider this your second home, sweetie," she said with a huge grin. "Now, let's clean up the kitchen. It's almost time for the news and Francy will be coming by soon."

The two quickly had the dirty dishes cleaned and put away. The smell of fresh brownies cooling on the counter made Lainey's stomach growl. When Vera walked into the living room to turn on the television, Lainey cut a tiny piece of brownie from one corner and gulped it down.

"Those darn corners are always burnt. Good thing you ate it before Mom took them to the station."

Lainey looked up to see Francy coming in the back door.

"Don't deny it. You have guilt written all over your face, and a few crumbs," she chuckled.

"They smelled so good. Vera won't be mad, will she?"

"She's used to us sneaking bites of her treats."

"Francy. Lainey. You'd better see this."

They walked into the living room to see Vera staring wide-eyed at the television screen.

The news anchor was saying, "Two people were killed in a crash on Hwy 23 between Mirror Falls and Paynesville. The utility vehicle, driven by Max Payton, was traveling at a high rate of speed when he apparently lost control and hit a concrete barrier causing his vehicle to burst into flames. His passenger, Herman Helvig, was thrown from the vehicle and was then struck by a vehicle that was traveling behind them. Payton, an area native, attended the University of Minnesota. Helvig was the retired president of Mirror Falls Bank and Trust and a respected philanthropist."

Vera turned the television off as Lainey stared in disbelief at the blank screen. Francy sat down on the couch, shaking her head. For a moment, the room was quiet.

"Did we hear that right? They're both dead?" Francy questioned. "I'm going to call the station. They may know more." She went into the kitchen to get her phone.

"This is bizarre, " Lainey said. "Helvig avoided detection for years and when he was about to be apprehended, he suddenly dies in car crash?"

"Don't look a gift horse in the mouth," Vera commented. "I'm never happy when people die, but those two horrible creatures got what they deserved. What goes around eventually comes around."

Francy came back into the room. "I didn't get much more information. Payton's body was badly burned, and they are waiting on autopsy and toxicology reports. The vehicle that hit Helvig was a gasoline tanker. He was crushed and partially dismembered."

"Wow, I'm stunned," Lainey said. "Guess I can go home now. There's no one left who would be listening anymore."

Vera nodded. "I'll come stay with you if you feel safer."

"Thank you, but I'll be fine. Powie's going to be stuck to me like glue for a while anyway." She gathered her things, walked to the front door and waved goodbye as she headed for her car.

"If I hear anything else, I'll let you know," Francy said.

"Don't forget our Whoopee dinner next Tuesday," Vera chimed in. "Della's making Lasagna!"

Lainey smiled as she got in her car. As she backed out of the driveway and headed to her house she said aloud, "I'm so glad I'm a Whoopee."

Powie was sleeping in front of the utility room door and began meowing and purring loudly when she walked in. She picked him up and walked into the kitchen and turned on the light. She gasped when she saw what was sitting on the counter. It was her backpack and her cell phone was lying next to it. She put down the cat and picked up the phone. There were no messages or missed calls.

She picked up the backpack and unzipped it. Her iPad was still inside and there was a small box in the bottom with a note taped to it. She opened the note and read in silence.

I wanted to make sure you recovered these items and to let you know that my family and I will be moving back to China in order to secure the family's business. We want to ensure it is not used for illegal purposes again. We have destroyed the evil enemy we came to defeat. Unfortunately, the price we had to pay was extremely high. I will grieve the loss of my daughter forever, but the women we were fortunate to rescue will help to fill the void in my heart. You're brave, intelligent, and strong-willed. I see a lot of my grandmother in you and that pleases me. Until we meet again, Miss A.

Lainey's eyes filled with tears as she put down the note and carefully opened the box. Inside was a red and gold velvet bag closed with a string tie. She loosened the tie, took the contents out, and gently set it on the counter. Jillian's golden Buddha statue glistened under the lights. Attached around its neck was a tiny red string with a small strip of red material attached. On the material were four words written in calligraphy… *Family Ties Run Deep.*

Want to know what adventure awaits Lainey and her friends?

Roommates

YOU CAN MAKE A DIFFERENCE

If you've enjoyed my book, please leave a review!
Curtain Call At Brooksey's Playhouse

Reviews are the most important and powerful ways to spread the word about my books.

I believe there is something more effective and personal than any type of ad.

It's you! Building a relationship with committed and loyal readers is powerful!

An honest review will help bring my books to other readers, something no amount of advertising can accomplish!

I humbly and gratefully ask you to spend a few minutes leaving a review if you enjoyed my book. It can be as short or long as you like.

Thank you and blessings on your day!

Laura Hern

ACKNOWLEDGMENTS

I am reminded daily how very blessed I am with family, friends, and readers who have provided so much support and encouragement! Thank you all!

My fabulous, award-winning cover designer, Linda Boulanger, once again created a masterpiece cover. Your talents are amazing.

My great appreciation to Grace Augustine, who is not only an editor extraordinaire, but an award winning writer and advocate for MS. I'm honored to be in your tribe.

Many thanks to Beth Raso, a voracious reader, outstanding organizer, editor, and friend. Your light hearted humor, invaluable insight, and encouragement brighten my day.

My family continue to lift me up with encouragement, ideas, and forgiveness for the many late night hours I spend sitting at my computer screen. I love you all.

And to my dear readers, you have my utmost thanks and gratitude. I always have you in my thoughts as I write each story. You are very special to me and I look forward to sharing with you for years to come.

Blessings,

Laura

ABOUT THE AUTHOR

Laura Hern writes cozy mysteries and romantic comedy. This is her third book in The Lainey Maynard Mystery series.

Her website is www.laurahern.com.

You can connect with Laura on her author Facebook page, on Twitter, and her website.

www.ingramcontent.com/pod-product-compliance
Lightning Source LLC
LaVergne TN
LVHW050959080826
845145LV00009B/2365

* 9 7 8 1 6 1 7 5 2 2 1 0 9 *